Let Your Lips Twitch

A Humorous Short Story Collection

Twitch

R.A. Clarke

PAGE TURN PRESS

You're the Best!!!!!
Enjoy ♡ xo

Published by Page Turn Press
9 Mellco Drive, Portage la Prairie, MB R1N 3Z5

Copyright © 2022 Rachael Clarke
Cover Design by Rachael Clarke (PTP Design).
Edited by Charlie Knight. Formatted by Steven Pajak.

Available in eBook and Paperback.
Print ISBN: 978-1-7771219-8-3
Epub ISBN: 978-1-7771219-9-0

www.pageturnpress.com

CONTENTS

To my Grandma, Ruby Rempel,
who always gave the best hugs.
I made sure to include #3 just for you.
Miss you and love you.

INTRODUCTION

If you've picked up this book, it's clear you're the type of person who enjoys a good chuckle. Or maybe it was just the bright cover that caught your attention? Either way, I have you here now, and you should most definitely read on.

Humour is something I adore. It's something that can sneak up on you, its construction wry or subtle. It can also smack you hard in the face, leaving you in stitches—the figurative kind, of course. Although now that I've said it, I wonder where that saying comes from? Hmm. Well, anyway, if by some bizarre happenstance humour leaves you needing *real* stitches, a: seek a doctor immediately, and b: use vitamin E to lessen the scar. Carrying on.

Laughter tends to tickle a person's funny bone, bubbling up from somewhere deep inside. The sheer power and simplicity of finding something funny is as beautiful as it is incomparable. Comedy can be shocking, heartwarming, gross, romantic, or cheeky. It may only whisper softly in the back of your mind. You can suppress amusement, but remnants always linger, watching and waiting to be triggered once more. Hilarity truly has no bounds, springing forth from darkness and light, and all shades in between.

Humour truly is everywhere. You only have to open your eyes and allow yourself to see it. To feel it. Let it settle into your bones and make a home there. When you do, you'll be rewarded with a unique sensation of buoyancy, dare I say joy, accompanied by an undeniable urge to smile. Your lips will twitch. The corners of your mouth will curl. You might even reveal teeth for all to see. Goodness knows, in this world we live in, we need more excuses to do that.

This book comprises a selection of works I have written with not only mirth in mind, but also variety. If you're curious to read about a jewel heist executed by a pair of bumbling thieves at a gastronomy party, a woman offered a chance to redo an all-consuming moment of regret, or a couple's high-tech scheme to set up their single friends, you're in the right place. These stories, like the others in this collection, encompass several genres, each one infused with unique characters, unbelievable situations, and even some fantasy.

Also, full disclosure. There's a teeny touch of potty humour in the mix. What can I say? I'm a mom of boys who find poop hilarious.

So, with that said, I invite you all to grab a cup of coffee, or tea, or whatever beverage soothes your soul, and curl up in a cozy place to read. My wish, as you flip through the pages of this short story collection, is simply this... Let yourself get drawn in, whisked away into exciting new worlds and experiences. Open yourself up to humour in all its glorious forms. Embrace it. Enjoy it.

Most of all, let your lips twitch.

Smiles will follow.

R.A. Clarke

NOW FOR
THE STORIES

A FRIEND IN NEED...

Kat

"Stop messing with my hair!" I swatted my best friend's hands away.

"Kat, I want you to look just right. You need to look exactly like your picture. Just wait—" Gloria tucked a few more stray hairs into my loose fishtail braid. "There. Perfect." She stood back, smiling.

"Ugh, I can't believe I let you talk me into this. I'm still mad at you. I hope you realize that." Best friends since college, Gloria and I were tied at the hip. She was like the sister I never had. Lately, we'd been having lunch together every day since her hair salon was only a block away from the bakery I recently bought.

She sighed, rolling her eyes skyward. "Yes, I imagine I'll be making up for this for a long time." Gloria grabbed our coats and waited for me by the door. "Ready to go? Don't want to be late."

"Maybe _you_ don't want to be late," I grumbled.

As we walked out of the apartment, she suddenly doubled back. Returning moments later, she held up a pair of black plastic-rimmed glasses. "Can't forget these. That would be a disaster."

"Right, because me going on a date pretending to be _you_ won't be a disaster enough?" I scoffed, then softened my scowl upon seeing her sombre expression. "Oh no, Gloria, I didn't mean it *that* way. You are one hundred percent wonderful—it's pretending to be you I'm struggling with. I just wish you'd been honest with this guy from the start." We headed to the stairwell.

"Well, hindsight is 20-20, right? Can't do anything about it now." Gloria flipped her chin-length blonde hair, the hurt look evaporating. "Trust me, this guy's worth it. If he's as nice as I suspect, then it'll be worth coming clean and taking the chance. *But* if he's a dick in person, I'll call you with some emergency, and we can bounce."

We jogged down the stairs and out the rear exit. "Alright, I guess that makes a little sense. *A little.*" I smirked when she cast a sidelong glance my way.

"It'll be fine, Kat. You wear the glasses, I'll feed you the information, and we'll be golden. Remember, my texts will show up on a tiny screen on the inside of your lens. Also, remember, his name is Steve. And your name is *Gloria.*"

We reached the car, slipping into our seats. I studied the glasses in my hand. "Where did you even get these things? Have you been a CIA agent all this time?" The sarcastic revelation made my friend snort with laughter.

"Can you imagine *me* as an *agent?* I can hardly tie my own shoes." She put the sedan in reverse, then guided us out of the parking lot. "No, I ordered them from a novelty shop. It's neat what a person can get their hands on nowadays."

"No kidding," I agreed, opening Steve's dating profile on my phone. The guy had green eyes, wavy chestnut hair, and dimples. I was a sucker for dimples. "Well, if he's really as good-looking as his picture, at least I'll have some eye candy for the evening."

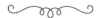

Lane

I CHUGGED MY DRINK, GLARING AT MY BUDDY STEVE WHILE we waited for *our* date at the bar. Sticking the tiny earpiece in place,

I winced when a loud squeal assaulted my eardrum. I pulled it back out, scowling.

"You're too close to me, Lane." Steve played with the matching device stuck in his own ear. "Just go sit at the table. Gloria's going to be here any minute." He waved me away, ignoring my death stares.

"You're lucky I like you so much," I growled, grabbing the second drink I'd ordered and heading to the table.

"And put your earpiece back in," he called out like a nagging mother.

Grudgingly, I complied. Seconds later, Steve's voice came through with only a slight echo.

"Check, check. Are you picking up what I'm putting down?"

I flipped him a thumbs up over my shoulder. "Loud and clear, Papa Bird. Can you hear me?"

"Roger, Baby Bird. We are a go for date night. The codename for Gloria will be GOOSE, got it?" His voice sounded aggravatingly cheerful. The guy had dragged me into his messy love life and was having far too much fun with it. I wondered if maybe this was just another way to escape the monotony of his accounting job. It made him good money, but I knew he hated it.

"Yeah, got it. Do we need all the codenames? I mean, we're not twelve years old." I sat down, setting the condensing glass of rum on the table. My stomach twisted with a sudden onset of nerves. Somehow, I had to play a convincing Steve for the night. Despite being *very* different individuals, we'd managed to stay friends since grade school, weathering college and beyond. We were almost thirty now, and Steve was still an impulsive extrovert—a life of the party type— while I was more of a homebody. Could I pull this off?

"Yes, we need the codenames. Because it's fun. Okay, things are working good, Baby Bird. I'll feed you whatever information you need as the night goes on. And don't drink too much. You get giggly when you're drunk."

"Right. But I'm only doing this one time. I want to be crystal clear on that. If you like this girl after today, you tell her the truth and let the chips fall where they may."

Steve went through a nasty divorce last year (the marriage was one of those impulse moves) and only recently dove back into the dating pool. Now, using my picture on his dating profile was a ridiculous, dead-headed move on his part—granted—but the guy kind of needed a win. That was the singular reason I agreed to go along with this mess of a plan he'd concocted.

"You forgot to say my codename," he pointed out.

Oh, for the love of...

"Baby Bird, the goose is cooked. I repeat, the goose is cooked!"

I sat up in my chair, swivelling to scan the foyer. The breath snagged in my throat when I spied a gorgeous woman with dark hair pulled into a loose braid walking in. A blonde entered right behind her, veering off to sit at the bar across from my friend. My focus returned to the woman I'd be sharing an evening with. She looked just like the picture Steve showed me. Except for the glasses. Those were new.

A hostess ushered the brunette to my table. I stood, smiling as she took off her coat and sat down across from me. *Gloria might be even prettier in person.* She wore light makeup, black patterned tights, and a navy top that hugged her curves. The atmospheric lights gave her brown eyes an almost golden hue. Sitting down again, I extended a hand across the table.

"Hello, I'm La-" I forced a cough, taking a quick sip of my drink before smoothing my smile. "So sorry, I find it quite dry in here. I'm *Steve*. Nice to finally meet you."

Gloria smiled back, shaking my hand with a firm grip. "Yes! It's nice to meet you, too. We've talked so much; I feel like we should've done this ages ago." She laughed and adjusted her rectangular glasses, glancing briefly toward the bar. We stared at each other awkwardly.

My throat felt as dry as the Sahara. My introverted ways definitely weren't helping me much in this situation. I couldn't even fall back on talking about work, which people usually found interesting. Nope, because she was here for Steve the accountant, not Lane the video game developer.

"Say something!" Steve chirped in my ear.

I felt like screaming back, *what do I say?* Handing my date a menu, I cleared my throat. "Have you eaten here before?"

"I haven't, actually. I've heard it's fantastic, though. And I like the decor." Her hand swept across the wall covered with quirky collectibles. She opened the menu. "You?"

"Me neither. Nope. Oh, and same—I've heard it's also good." I groaned inwardly. Clearly, I lacked the ability to put together a coherent sentence. Nodding uncomfortably, we both looked down at our menus.

"What is wrong with you?" It sounded like Steve was fighting laughter. **"Just ask about her dog, Trixie."**

Finally, something helpful. "So, Gloria, how's Trixie doing?"

She looked up, her face brightening. "Oh, Trixie! Yes, my dog. She's doing great. You know, just your typical everyday poodle—" Gloria adjusted her glasses, brows pinching together. "Or, Bichon. Sorry, I meant Bichon. I can't speak today, apparently." She chuckled at herself.

I grinned. "Hey, it's all good. I know the feeling. I'm not going to lie; I feel a little nervous right now."

Gloria brightened even more. "You too? Oh, thank goodness I'm not alone." She closed her menu, folding her hands together on the table. "That makes me feel a lot better. Talking in person is just so much different from typing on a computer, you know?"

"Absolutely. One hundred percent agree." I took a sip of my drink, then lowered my voice, leaning in. "You're also beautiful, which doesn't help matters." Go big or go home, right? It was true, so why not say it? Steve probably would have. A touch of pink graced her cheeks.

"Nice work, Baby Bird. Now we're getting somewhere."

The waitress came by to take our order, and we continued somewhat stunted chatter while we awaited our food. It wasn't an award-winning conversation, but it slowly got easier. Steve kept throwing things at me whenever there was the slightest pause—random information I had to scramble to make something out of. Like, just a minute ago, he'd said, **"She loves pizza. Talk about pizza."** Not exactly a romantic conversation starter, but I'd salvaged the very unspecific suggestion by boldly suggesting a pizza joint for date number two.

"I mean, you *are* a pizza lover, right? Is my memory correct?" I quickly added, wiping my increasingly sweaty palms on my pants.

"You're correct. I definitely am. I actually consider pizza its own food group." She giggled.

The sound was infectious. I couldn't help but chuckle along. "It's nice to meet a woman with a healthy appetite. So, what's your favourite kind? Name your toppings."

"Let me think." Gloria tapped her chin, her eyes crossing as if she was trying to read something too close to her face. Then they normalised again. "I'll have to go with ham and pineapple—nothing too crazy." The waiter appeared with a water jug, topping up our glasses.

I nodded, leaning back and crossing my arms over my chest. "I respect that decision. My first choice would be Canadian, but ham and pineapple is right up there on the list, too."

"Canadian. Nice." Gloria's eyes crossed again right before she announced she needed to sneak off to the little girl's room. As I watched her walk away, I couldn't help but admire the view. Then I shook my head, snapping out of it. Gloria was Steve's girl. *Chill out, Lane.*

"The coast is clear. Come to the bar for a minute."

I did as he asked, leaning against the counter with a heavy sigh. After flagging the bartender, I ordered another rum. I didn't care if booze made me giggly. I'd take that over awkward any day.

"So? What do you think of her?" Steve asked expectantly. "It seems to be going alright."

"Are you serious? I mean, she's pretty and super nice—so great job there—but it feels like I'm crashing and burning. *Hard.* Do you have enough information by now to make your decision? I'd be fine with making up some random reason to leave right now."

"You want to leave? The night's just getting started." Steve's gaze flitted past me to the blonde across the bar. The slightest hint of a smile played on his lips. My eyes swung to the mystery woman capturing his interest. Her eyes dropped to her phone, madly texting with someone.

I leaned in to whisper, "What's with the blonde?"

Steve flashed a grin. "Cute, isn't she?"

My head rolled atop my shoulders, my brows practically stretching into my hairline. "Did you just say she's cute? Um, what about Gloria? You know, the girl you've been dating online for months? The girl we're meeting *tonight*." I enunciated every word.

"Hey, there's no harm in looking, my friend," Steve winked, taking a big swig of his beer. "Don't worry. By the end of tonight, I'll know enough to decide about Gloria. Just like we discussed. It's all good. Just relax and try to enjoy the evening, will ya?" He patted my shoulder.

I bit back a groan of frustration. Here I was busting my balls to get in the good books with his supposed dream woman, and the whole time he's been sitting here making eyes at someone else. My fists clenched by my sides. "Just remember the mission, Steve." I turned, walking back to the table. Our food was arriving, and I spied Gloria round the corner from the restrooms.

"Duck, duck, goose!" Steve shouted in my ear, the reverberation making me wince. I smoothed the front of my shirt and ran a hand through my hair, preparing for round two.

Here we go. You got this.

Kat

MY PHONE BUZZED IN MY POCKET, AND I PAUSED TO CHECK it before reaching the table.

G: Kat, this guy at the bar just ordered me a drink. Adorbs, hey?

Adorbs? Shooting her a glare, I madly typed a message in return.

K: What the hell? Tell him to bugger off. You're here for Steve.

Speaking of Steve...he was looking at me right now. I gave a little wave and held up a pointer finger with an apologetic look. He mouthed for me to go ahead, seemingly unconcerned. Gosh, the man had a brilliant smile. I had to commend Gloria's taste on this one. He was handsome and seemed sweet, albeit a bit awkward— but that wasn't a deal-breaker. Likely nervous. This was a first date, after all. I remained determined to put my best foot forward for my friend's sake, hoping this could work out for her. Her string of loser boyfriends seriously needed to end. It was high time she landed a good one. Even if it made me a little jealous.

G: I will. Just go do your thing. Switching messaging back to the spy glasses now.

K: Ok.

I tucked the phone away. We'd been messaging the entire time I was in the bathroom. Most of Gloria's messages revolved around determining if I liked or approved of Steve. Once, she even asked if I'd consider dating him if the tables were turned, which was a touch odd. I told her he seemed great, but it wasn't *me* who needed to decide that. However, whenever I asked for *her* thoughts—whether she knew what she'd do yet—the woman remained vague. It was irritating, but I pushed it aside, already having spent too much time in the bathroom.

I sat back down at the table with Steve and smiled. "Hi again. Did I miss anything important?"

He grinned back. "Nothing but food. You have perfect timing. It just arrived." He stabbed a forkful of a salad slathered with Italian dressing.

"Oh good, because I'm hungry." Slicing my enormous chicken burger in half, I attempted to take ladylike bites. Even still, globs of sauce oozed out. I couldn't help but grimace—not because of the mess but from tasting the bland flavour in the bun. *Man, the ones from my bakery could crush these any day of the week.* On the inner lens of my glasses, a tiny screen suddenly flashed back to life. I pretended to focus on my meal, all the while straining to read each minuscule word as they scrolled across. Could the screen be any smaller? Thank goodness I had 20-20 vision, or else it would be game over.

Gloria's message read: ***I must find out if he's serious. Why don't you hold his hand? See what happens.***

Was she kidding? I didn't agree to anything physical. Pretending to stretch, I scowled over at her, shaking my head ever so slightly.

Do it. I need to know if he's worth the headache.

I was really starting to despise her right now. While I silently fumed, another message came.

Do you think they'll hate us for this? I'm having second thoughts.

What? Who will hate who?

Oops, sorry, wrong person.

Suspicion seeped into my consciousness. *Who else is she texting with?*

"So, Gloria," Steve's cheerful voice interrupted my thoughts. He'd been watching me with an odd expression on his face, like he was trying to figure something out. But then he replaced that look with one of interest, continuing. "From what you've said in the past, you have a passion for abstract art. Can you tell me more about this? Who's your favourite artist?"

"Oh, art? Yes, of course. I adore abstract art." I waited, an awkward pause growing between us. Words should've been scrolling before my eyes by now, yet nothing came. Out of desperation, I blurted, "The colours! The paint. It's all so...abstract." Laughing nervously, I tapped my glasses, hoping to get things working again. Were they broken? *C'mon, c'mon.*

Steve tilted his head with a bemused chuckle, brows slightly furrowed. "Um, yes. That it is. And your favourite artist?" He stared at me, waiting for elaboration.

Pushing the glasses higher on my nose, my eyes skittered toward the bar in panic. Instant rage exploded as I spied my co-conspirator chatting with another man—one who looked like a shorter, paler second cousin to Vin Diesel. They sat two seats apart, and I presumed this was the same guy who'd bought her the drink. My gaze zoomed in on her phone, ignored on the countertop.

"Gloria?" Steve leaned forward. "Are you okay? Are your glasses bugging you?"

"Uh," I stammered, unclenching my jaw. "They are, actually. How observant of you. I just got this pair yesterday—a new prescription. It's been hard adjusting." *Whew, okay, that's plausible.*

"Shoot, that's unfortunate. They could've gotten the prescription wrong. Or perhaps they just need adjusting? Here, let me have a look at them. I actually used to work at an optometrist's office for a while after high school." Steve smiled helpfully, reaching across the table. His outstretched hands zeroed in on my glasses.

"No." I recoiled sharply, bumping a knee on the table, which in turn spilled my glass. An involuntary squeal escaped my lips as icy liquid splashed onto my lap. Steve jerked his hands back in alarm before snatching up his napkin and taking action to stem the water's flow.

While he madly patted the table, I stood, cheeks flaming. "I'm so sorry," I stammered, brushing at the water already soaked into my tights. "I don't know what happened there." Patrons were staring. Gloria and her boy toy watched with mouths agape. My friend must've sensed my desperation because she finally grabbed her phone. On cue, letters scrolled before my eyes.

Bathroom break. Meet you there.

"Uh, I need to dry myself off. I'll be back in a minute. I'm such a klutz. Sorry again," I mumbled, turning away. Before Steve could even reply, I'd already rushed off. I couldn't wait to get Gloria alone and tear a strip off of her. She clearly wasn't taking this seriously at all, and all I was doing was making an ass of myself in front of this poor man who had no clue what he'd signed up for. *I'm calling the whole thing off. It ends now.*

Lane

A WAITER CAME TO THE TABLE WITH MORE NAPKINS, offering to reset the table, but I didn't think that was necessary. This charade was over. I asked for the check and a box to pack my food in.

"What are you doing, Lane?" Steve asked in my ear.

"Going home," I replied bluntly. Standing, I grabbed my coat. As soon as Gloria came back, I'd politely explain that an emergency popped up, and I needed to leave. Easy.

"No, you can't give up! You guys were finally starting to gel."

"Gel? She was so appalled by the very thought of me touching her that she spazzed and spilled water everywhere. I wouldn't say that's *gelling*. Something weird is going on here." I ignored the curious looks other diners gave me—the nut job having a conversation with nobody. Growling, I stalked to the bar.

Steve had his hands up in defence before I even got there. He knew I was pissed.

"Look, bud, I thought you'd really like her, I swear. Don't kill me." He winced, leaning away.

Stopping beside his stool, I loomed over him. "Don't you mean you thought *you'd* really like her?" The flirtatious blonde I'd seen him chatting up had disappeared, her purse and jacket still slung over her chair. There's no way a woman would leave her personal things behind like that unless she trusted the person she'd left them with. Crossing my arms, I levelled my gaze. "Okay, what is going on? For real? Who's the girl?" I jerked my head toward the recently vacated seat.

Steve downed his drink, locking eyes with me. "Alright, but don't get mad."

"Spit it out."

"I wasn't lying when I said I've been dating a girl named Gloria online for months." Steve took a deep breath. "But...*Gloria* has been sitting here at the bar the whole time." He cringed, waiting.

"Wait—her name's Gloria too?" My brows furrowed, my mind spinning as it tried to connect the dots. I noticed a middle-aged woman with flaming red hair waiting for a drink at the bar. She snuck furtive glances our way, trying her best to act disinterested. Had I somehow been trapped inside a tele-novella—the whole bloody lounge now watching with popcorn in hand?

"No." Steve pointed to the empty stool two down from him. "*This* is Gloria. The only one. The woman you actually met is Katherine."

Running a hand through my wavy chestnut hair, I leaned against the counter. "What? Who's Katherine now? What is going on?"

Steve motioned for the bartender to bring two more drinks. "Sit." He waited until I'd settled before continuing. "Remember when I said you need to get out more?"

Stifling a groan, I sliced him a glare, already not liking the sound of where this was headed. "So? Go on."

"Well, Gloria, my *girlfriend*, who I already met a month ago—" he said precisely, letting each word sink in. "—told me one night she had a cute friend named Katherine who seemed perfect for you. I guess one thing led to another, and here we are."

The drinks arrived. My supposed friend slid one over to me, but I ignored it, my eyes unwavering from his face. His scheming, manipulative face. "This was all a setup?"

With a nervous smile, Steve clinked his glass to mine, then took a big swig. "Cheers."

Kat

"YOU WHAT?" I SHOUTED, THEN REELED IT IN WHEN A TOILET flushed—quickly remembering the lady who'd slipped into a bathroom stall a minute earlier. "You what?" I hissed.

"I'm sorry, Kat! We thought it would be fun. Then it became not-so-fun. From what Steve said, the guy sounded perfect for you. But he also said Lane would never agree to go on a blind date, and I definitely *knew* you wouldn't." She paused as the occupied stall door opened. A middle-aged woman with flaming red hair stepped to the sink to wash her hands.

I leaned in close, whispering, "Damn straight, I wouldn't. Because I'm perfectly capable of finding my own men to date."

Gloria's eyes flicked to the lady who was trying—very poorly—to hide the fact she was listening in. Muttering quietly, my friend continued, "You just proved my point. There was no other way to get you and him together. And he's a genuinely nice guy. You deserve a nice guy. Besides, you can't possibly deny Lane is attractive. Why not just give him a chance?"

I groaned, waving her words away before leaning on the smooth quartz counter. "I still can't wrap my head around how you guys came up with this bizarre scheme in the first place? I mean, did you make fake profiles just for this?"

The hint of a smile played on Gloria's lips. "Well, yes. Steve and I met on that dating site, and look how great it turned out? We're dating now, and he's amazing."

I huffed, staring at my disastrous reflection in the mirror. A round wet patch circled my groin. My braid was falling apart—hair sticking out everywhere. "Whose idea was it?"

Gloria wrung her hands. "A kind of team effort, I guess. One night Steve just made an offhand joke about using our dating platform to set you up, then jokes led to plans..." She shrugged. "We just wanted to get you both in the same room to see what happened."

The woman at the sink was taking an exorbitantly long amount of time to wash her hands. I turned my back to her, facing my friend. "I just can't believe you did this. It's so disrespectful. I genuinely wanted to help you; you know? Wanted you to snag a great guy. Then I was furious when you cozied up to that man at the bar, abandoning me. And now...I just want to kill you!"

"Steve. *That man's* name is Steve."

"Fine. Steve. I mean, how could you even think that Link and I—"

"Not Link. His name is Lane."

"Whoever!" I growled, hands shaking. "How could you even think *Lane* and I could truly get to know each other while we're busy pretending to be *you guys* the whole time?" My voice rose again. Our eavesdropper nodded while lathering up her third squirt of soap.

Gloria grew quiet as her posture deflated. "Yeah...we didn't really think that part through—that's true." Then she shot up, giving a finger wag. "But you can't deny you're attracted to him."

"Ugh!" Spinning away from her, I ran my hands over my face. "I just can't believe this."

The red-haired woman finally shut off the tap, then dried her hands on paper towels as she sauntered past us. She paused beside me for a second, leaning in like a coach pep-talking an exhausted pitcher with bases loaded. "Sounds like their intentions came from a good place, honey. If he's a catch, I'd snatch him up." Then, with a firm nod, she carried on out the door.

Gloria and I stared after her, exchanging a glance before bursting into laughter. Moments later, when the room fell silent once more, my friend laid a hand on my arm. Voice soft, she asked, "Will you at least come meet him for real this time? No alter-egos. Just you and him."

I sighed, searching her eyes while I searched my heart. He did seem really nice. "Gosh, he probably thinks I'm crazy now. Does he know the jig is up?"

Gloria whipped out her phone, sending a text to her new beau. "If he didn't before, he does now."

I smoothed my shirt, trying to pull it lower to cover the water mark on my pants. "So, the message I got—the one you sent to the wrong person—that was to the *real* Steve?"

"Yeah. Remember when I told you in the car how I could never be CIA? Case and point." She giggled, and I couldn't help but join in.

"Covert is definitely not your strong suit." I pulled out my lip balm, applying a fresh layer. "Especially since you two couldn't even stay away from each other long enough to see the plan through. When I saw you sitting closer to him at the bar, I just knew something was off." As I tucked wayward wisps of hair back into my braid, I gave a wry grin.

Gloria shrugged unapologetically. "What can I say? He just revs my engines. Can't get enough."

Despite myself, I let out a snort of laughter.

"So, will you come?" Her eyes had grown hopeful watching me freshen up. "And can you forgive me? I'm *so thankful* you wanted to help me out, and I'm sorry it ended up like this."

I released a long, resigned sigh. Then I nodded. "Yes, I'll come meet him. And yeah, I'm sure I'll be able to forgive you—eventually." One corner of my mouth curled upward.

"That's good enough for me. Let's go."

Lane

"Besides the fact that I still want to punch you right now..." I leaned back in my chair. "I'll admit your plan was somewhat masterful. Even if poorly executed."

Steve spread his arms wide. "Right?"

"I mean, all of that just to drag me out of the house?" I shook my head. "Incredible."

"There's no other way it was going to happen, Lane. Your last real relationship was three years ago. Now, I know she wrecked you good, but you need to get back on the horse."

I stared at my finger tracing the rim of my glass. "The horse bucked me off."

Steve grabbed my shoulder, shaking me. "Lane, this is a brand-new horse. A fresh chance. I'm only thinking of your best interests."

Stretching the stress from my neck, I scanned the lounge. Groups of friends and couples sat around, chatting. A collection of people cheered as their team scored on the big screen TV. I suppose I had been a bit distant from everyday life. Aside from the occasional outing with friends, my focus revolved around work and my dog. Without realising it, my social life had shrivelled.

"You alright?" Steve asked.

"Yeah, I'm fine." I shook the thoughts away. "All I gotta say is, you owe me *big* after this."

Steve raised a hand like he was taking a solemn oath. "Big. Yep. Duly noted."

"What a cluster." I groaned.

"But was it worth it? Was *she* worth it? I have to say, everything Gloria told me about Katherine seems to be spot on."

I shrugged. "Whether she's *worth it* is yet to be determined. I have no clue who she really is at this point." I levelled my gaze. "Is she interesting, though? Absolutely." I downed the last few gulps of my drink, then slammed it down. "But now, the big question is, has she run for the hills?"

"*She* has not," a familiar female voice announced behind me. Steve and I spun on our stools; eyes wide. There stood Katherine—sans glasses—with Gloria right beside her. *How long were they standing there?*

"The goose has flown south," Steve mumbled before breaking into a wide grin. "Ladies!" He reached out and pulled Gloria to his side, adding, "Hi, babe." They kissed.

I swallowed hard, nerves hitting me all over again. This time, in a very different way. I no longer felt the pressure of having to adequately play a role. Now I had to show the real me and try not to sound like a real idiot in front of a pretty girl. These feelings were the prime reason I didn't go out much. If you don't stick your neck out, it doesn't get sliced. But that had to change.

"Hello again," I said with a wave.

"Hi," Katherine—not Gloria—replied. She was smiling at least. The same shy variety I likely had plastered on my face. Our eyes locked a fraction longer than necessary before we turned away.

"Well now, wasn't that a crazy string of events? Hey guys?" Steve blurted to keep things moving along. He and Gloria shared a knowing look before her elbow nudged his ribs.

"It sure was!" Gloria exclaimed; her words somewhat over-exaggerated. She stretched out her arms, yawning. "Man, I'm bushed. Will you drive me home, Steve?"

He nodded, picking up on the not-so-subtle cue.

I rolled my eyes skyward.

"Will you two be able to find your way home? Or should we call you a cab?" Steve asked. He helped Gloria put on her coat, then shrugged on his own.

"We'll be fine," I assured, with a dry smile.

"You two lovebirds have a good night," Katherine called sweetly to the trouble-making couple as they headed for the door.

Gloria winked. "You too."

Kat

I CLAIMED THE STOOL BESIDE LANE. "SO, WHAT KIND OF high-tech gadget were you guys using?"

He laughed, digging into his pocket and presenting a tiny earpiece. "It's not as high-tech as one might think."

"Impressive." I brandished my glasses, setting them on the bar. Waving my hands like Vanna White, I announced, "Ta-dah!"

Lane picked up the glasses to inspect them more closely. "Very nice. All the pieces are coming together now. I wondered what was up with your glasses. For one, you weren't wearing any in the picture I saw. For two, you flipped out when I even dared to try touching them." We both laughed, remembering the ordeal.

I shrugged sheepishly, somewhat embarrassed. "Yep, real elite spy stuff." Taking the glasses from his hands, I put them on and struck a pose, complete with pouty lips. He nodded in approval, then reached to slip them off my face again. Lane's fingers brushed my cheeks, and a barrage of warm tingles assaulted my stomach.

"I think you missed your true calling," Lane said. "Spy or model, you could go either way."

The heat spread to my cheeks. "Wow, you're a charmer, aren't you?"

He grinned, eyes twinkling. "Only when I want to be."

Lane's dimples were on full display, and I was there for it. He ordered us drinks, and we continued to chat. Now that the ruse was over with, we could finally be ourselves. The man spoke with sincerity, loved his family and his dog, and revealed he's a bit of a workaholic—not unlike myself. I could tell there were layers to Lane. And the more time we spent together, the more I wanted to peel them away one by one.

"So, how do these work anyway?" he finally asked, holding out the glasses again.

Pointing at the lens, I explained, "A person with a paired device types a message, and it's displayed on a tiny screen right here." Our hands touched, neither of us quick to pull away.

"Huh. Neat." A mischievous smile curled his lips. "Somehow, I don't think an actual spy would use these, though."

"Oh?" Sipping my cocktail, I casually glanced around the room. The same red-haired woman from the bathroom sat in a nearby booth. She happened to meet my gaze, flashed an approving grin and a thumbs up. I stifled a laugh, almost choking on my drink.

"Are you okay?" Lane asked, his hand coming to rest on my back.

I shook my head, reclaiming my ability to speak. "Yeah, totally fine. Sorry. I saw someone I know over there." Lane's brows raised, curious. "It's nothing, really. So, you were saying?"

His hand moved off my back, though I wished it hadn't. Lane proceeded to put the glasses on himself, looking bookish in an alarmingly attractive way.

"I don't think you realized you were doing this, but whenever you got messages, your eyes would kind of cross—like this." Lane pulled his irises inward. "Most of the time, you were looking around or down, so I didn't see it. But a couple of times...yeah, it had me wondering. It's funny now that I know the full story." With a chuckle, he took them off again.

"Really? Oh, no," I moaned. "Can I melt into my shoes and disappear now?" Slamming both elbows down, I buried my face in my hands. Lane's laugh deepened, the rich tone wrapping around me like a warm hug. His hand settled on my back again, rubbing lightly back and forth.

"No, no melting allowed." He gently pried the fingers away from my face, regaining eye contact. His next words were reassuring. "Honestly, it was cute." Lane's hand lingered on mine, and with a burst of bravery, I laced my fingers between his. We shared a slow smile.

There were those tingles again.

Abruptly, Lane cleared his throat and pulled away. "Okay, listen. I think there's something important we need to do here." Standing up, he smoothed his shirt and hair. "You too, stand up."

I followed his instruction, eyeing him curiously. "What are we doing?"

"Hold out your hand. Like this, c'mon," he urged, holding out his own.

Sensing what he might be getting at, I tentatively mirrored the motion.

"We need a fresh start." Lane's smile beamed playfully as he shook my hand. "Hello, my name is Lane. I must say, I think you're a beautiful woman, and it's my pleasure to meet you."

I broke into giggles, heat flaming on my cheeks. "Flattery will get you everywhere, kind sir." Our surroundings seemed to fade away as this adorable man captured my full attention. Clearing my throat, I quickly straightened my expression. It was my turn. "Well, hello, Lane. Now *I must say*, the pleasure is all mine. My name is Katherine—not Gloria. However, you can just call me Kat."

Amusement gleamed in Lane's eyes. Gently, he brushed an errant lock of hair behind my ear, then lifted the back of my hand to his lips. He placed a kiss there, feather-light.

We both stilled, the moment suspended in time.

"Kat. I like that."

SHELF HELP

"Look, FindingFortune is back!"

Excited murmurs flew as Mrs. Frintle, our kindly grey-haired librarian, slid a familiar green book onto a shelf opposite mine.

Six walnut shelving units comprised the self-help section I called home, three on each side, creating a tunnel of solace for needy readers. I happened to be perched smack in the middle, second from the top.

"Hey, stranger! Long time no see. You get checked out so much, we hardly ever see you anymore," I called to the ever-popular volume. He'd been overdue for weeks.

"Hello, Rewire! Yes, it's been quite a while. I've been swamped—money matters, you know. Everyone wants to make a buck." FindingFortune greeted his neighbours with cheerful spine bumps.

Though *Rewire Your Brain: Conquer Addiction, Bad Habits & Destructive Behaviours* was my full name, everyone in the self-help section just called me Rewire. I considered myself lucky to be part of this tight-knit community. We celebrated and commiserated together, regardless of our vast differences. I don't know what I would've done if my author had penned me into a horror. Those books were constantly at each other's throats, out for blood.

My best friend, *Live Envy Free,* leaned in. "Geez, that dude gets so much action. Must be nice."

"No kidding." I watched as the alluring GirlYou'reWorthIt shuffled along the shelf to squeeze in beside FindingFortune, their pages fluttering instantly.

Action in more ways than one.

I looked away, giving my buddy a nudge. "Hey, I don't get pulled much either, man. You're not alone."

"What are you talking about? Stubby pulls you all the time," EnvyFree muttered.

Stubby was our nickname for the short, thick-fingered man who reliably whisked me away every month or so. Despite the fact self-help books are printed specifically to help *many* people, I considered Stubby my person. That wasn't his real name, though. Repeat borrowers always earned special callsigns. Like BoozeBeGone's faithful 12-stepper we called Tipsy, or SociallyAwkward's introverted writer, Mouse.

I scoffed. "Well, okay, sure. But I mean, it's not exactly a *legit* pull when someone steals you." Stubby's thick fingers were also very sticky—a grifter by trade.

The door chimed; a melodic telltale signal borrowers were incoming. Wonderful. It had been a quiet day at the library so far.

With school out for summer, people were off enjoying the sunshine. The parks were likely packed. Oh, how I loved to be read beneath the sprawling canopies there, warm rays brightening my pages. Stubby and I even had our own special tree.

"A pull is a pull, man." EnvyFree let out a pained sigh. "Why aren't there more jealous people in the world?"

A spider scurried past, and I tipped my spine in greeting before looking back at EnvyFree. "I bet there are plenty. Maybe they're just not ready to face it yet, ya know?"

"Maybe." Then EnvyFree perked up, as though he'd remembered something important. "Hey, speaking of Stubby, shouldn't he have shown up by now?"

"Yeah, it's been *well* over a month since he brought me back last time. Who knows, maybe he finally kicked his addiction." A bittersweet mixture of emotion settled in my binding. The man had been struggling to go straight for so long. Of course, it would be wonderful if he finally found success. Even so, I missed our time together when he was away. He always read my pages so thoroughly. Made me feel useful—appreciated.

What if he doesn't come back?

"Incoming!" a book named BetterLover bellowed from his lookout.

A middle-aged woman wearing large round glasses appeared, brows knitted together as she scanned spine after spine.

"Ooooh, she looks like she's got mommy-daddy issues," Child-hoodToxicity purred, subtly pushing herself out an inch as the lady approached. "Let me ease your feelings of abandonment. You are worthy!"

The woman paused, lingering in front of ChildhoodToxicity's shelf for a moment. Her contemplative gaze sent the entire row into a frenzy. Rapid fire pitches flew through the air.

"Do you need to remember your spirit?"

"I can show you the path to success!"

"Looks like you could lose a few pounds—let me make that happen!"

"Struggling with your partner's sexual dysfunction? I'll help you deal with it!"

But as with most humans, our words were beyond perception. Only charmed individuals could comprehend this library's living energy. People like our librarian, Mrs. Frintle. With a shake of her head, the woman carried on, leaving a collective chorus of groans in her wake.

"She'll be back. She sees your value. She'll be back. She sees your value." ChildhoodToxicity repeated the mantra over and over to herself.

I felt bad for her. It had been ages since someone checked her out. What a letdown. Suddenly, I felt even more thankful for my regular reader...and simultaneously more worried he might not return.

"Hey, ChildhoodToxicity," a grumpy book with tattered pages

called from the far end of the aisle. "Your incessant muttering is hurting my ears. Why don't you read a few of Acceptance's chapters, and *MOVE ON*."

"Oh, snap shut, will you AngerManagement?" she shot back, in no mood to put up with his attitude. "Why don't *you* take a lesson from MaximumMeditation and *chill out.*"

AngerManagement flipped her a middle page, and she huffed. "Go fall off a shelf."

Books shuffled uncomfortably, avoiding involvement. When Anger was riled up, it was hard to calm him down again. A difficult title sometimes, but deep down, we all knew he meant well—as passionate about helping people as the rest of us. For that reason, we put up with him.

EnvyFree gasped beside me.

"What's going on?" I asked, looking back at my friend. That's when I realized the woman in glasses had stopped in front of our shelf. "Oh..."

"Please pick me..." Envy Free whispered, shaking so much his pages might wrinkle.

Her fingers caressed our titles, reading aloud. "*Unfunk Your Brain, Keys to Unlocking Self Esteem, Living Envy Free.* Hmm..." Then her finger settled on my spine, and I fought to keep myself from quivering. Though I really didn't want anybody but Stubby to pull me, there was always a certain thrill that accompanied being considered.

But with a quick nose scrunch, she continued meandering.

"Runny ink. I thought she might pull one of us for a second," EnvyFree grumbled. If he had shoulders, they would've sagged.

I patted his cover. "Oh, well. Maybe next time."

The chime sounded again, light flashing across the faded green carpets as the door opened and closed. At least business was picking up. A family of four flitted toward the children's section, followed by a short-stature man in a black baseball cap.

Yes! I recognized those thick fingers immediately. "Stubby's here. I'm sure he'll be by pretty soon." *Thank goodness.* Like always, he'd make the usual rounds, casually perusing random aisles to avoid suspicion—even though all the librarians were wise to his game.

What a relief the bespectacled lady hadn't picked me. How horrible would it have been if I wasn't here for him to pull? Sure, having a new reader would be fun, but Stubby relied on me. It was my obligation to help him with his problems.

"His ears must've been burning," EnvyFree said.

A sudden onset of heavy breathing stole our attention down the row. Tipping forward, I spied an excitable book named Punting-Panic entering full hyperventilation mode. The middle-aged woman had picked her up to read her blurb.

"Guys, I don't know if I can do this!" she cried. "What if she puts me in her bag? You know I hate confined spaces. Or what if she hates me? What if—"

"You've got this girl!" a hardcover named TimeToShine cut off the anxiety-ridden paperback's words before she could escalate any further. "Just be the book you were bound to be!"

"Right...okay. Okay."

Several agonizing moments later, the woman snapped Punting-Panic shut and headed to the check-out counter, book in hand. A resounding cheer rose from the section as the pair vanished around the corner. I smiled. *Good for her.*

"Well, at least someone got picked," EnvyFree said. "Wish it was me, though."

I gave his cover a pat. "You're not alone, my friend. Not alone."

Sneaking peeks at the aisle opening, a growing impatience saturated my fibres. *C'mon, Stubby. Where are you?*

Mrs. Frintle happened to come walking down the row, smiling as she passed. "Guess what? I have a new friend for you," she whispered to nobody in particular. Such a sweet lady. One of the few charmed humans who could understand us books—an ability passed down from her mother, a white witch. She'd dedicated much of her time to this library. Since her husband passed years ago, she needed something to keep busy. And to her, we were more than just books. We were friends. I'd never say this aloud, for fear of upsetting the other gifted librarians, but Mrs. Frintle was my favourite.

Her slightly crooked fingers placed the new book on a nearby shelf. "Have fun getting to know each other," she chirped quietly, eyes as bright as her smile. And with that, she left us to our curiosity.

"Who are you?" a saddle-stitch named SpeakUp shouted, surprising no one.

I craned my spine to get a look at the thick, blue-covered book shuffling forward to present herself. She looked pretty nervous.

"Hi, I'm *Live Phobia Free: Finding Relief from Fear that Plagues You*, but you can just call me PhobiaFree. It's nice to meet all of you."

A myriad of greetings rippled from the shelves, and the new book gave a shy smile.

EnvyFree nudged my cover. "Oh man, check her out. She's a real page turner."

I grinned. "Probably has a nice preface."

Then a page-ripping scream sliced the air.

"Oh, my ink! Is that a spider?" PhobiaFree shrieked again, recoiling from one of the many arachnids that called this library home. The poor thing had slipped down to meet her, but now startled, it zoomed back up his wispy thread at lightning speed.

Words came tumbling from the terrified book in a rush. "Arachnophobia is the extreme or irrational fear of spiders. Symptoms may include emotional outbursts, sweating, trouble breathing, nausea, and heart palpitations. Relaxation techniques and exposure therapy are common treatment options."

"Hey, don't be afraid, PhobiaFree." Speaking in an even tone, EnvyFree attempted to soothe her. "Try to relax. That's just Newton. He lives here and loves to read—part of the family."

PhobiaFree took a few deep breaths, locking eyes with EnvyFree. "Ooookay, I'll try. Thank you...er, what's your name?" PhobiaFree flashed a shaky, yet adorable smile, and I could practically hear my friend's heart melting beside me.

"I'm EnvyFree. And any time."

I didn't need to read between the lines to know they'd be asking Mrs. Frintle for a romantic ride on the book cart soon enough.

"Incoming!" BetterLover's alarm sounded.

Gazes snapped back to the aisle entrance as a male form approached. Head bowed; the mysterious fellow hid a clean-shaven face beneath the curved brim of a ball cap. However, within a few quick seconds, everyone realized who it was.

Stubby.

He sidled up to my shelf, unzipping his flannel jacket halfway. His fingers hovered as his eyes scanned for any sign the librarian might approach.

"Hey, Rewire. You think he's a chapter shy of a full index? I mean, he *does* know he can just check you out, right?" EnvyFree asked with a chuckle.

"Oh, he does. But the poor guy can't help it. You already know why—he's a con-man desperate to quit the con. We're working on it."

Sadly, his need to steal and swindle ran deep. It was the same routine every time. He stole me, read me, went through a period of self-loathing and repentance, then felt guilty for thieving and snuck me back into the library.

Stubby's fingers slipped around my matte charcoal cover, pausing as Mrs. Frintle sauntered down the aisle to shelve a few returned books. The woman gave me a knowing wink when he wasn't looking, then hummed her way down the row. She knew I'd be back.

"Gotta hand it to him. He's dedicated," EnvyFree said. "What makes him want to quit so badly?"

"His grandmother raised him—made him promise to give it up before she passed away. He's got no other family." Like all books, I sensed my readers' emotions while being read, and every time Stubby came for me, he was riddled with chronic guilt over his failure to straighten out. He craved the wisdom and encouragement printed within my pages.

"Shoot, now I feel bad for making that index joke." EnvyFree paused. "I still don't get why he doesn't just keep you, though." My friend quickly added, "Not that I want that! I'd miss you, buddy."

"I know. Same here." The librarian disappeared from view, and I spoke faster, running out of time. "Essentially, keeping me goes against everything he's trying to achieve...yet stealing me is like a comfort blanket. It's a vicious cycle of addiction."

Honestly, though, I really didn't care if I got borrowed or stolen, as long as I got to be with Stubby.

"Geez, no kidding. Well, he's got the right book for the job," EnvyFree said, then laughed. "Hey, for once, I'm not jealous!"

I chuckled as my personal thief finally lifted me from the shelf, opening his jacket wider. This was it. *Go time.* "I'll see you soon, EnvyFree. If all goes to plan—a few weeks, max!"

"That's right, Rewire! Have faith in your abilities! Be the light!" PowerfulPositivity cried from the shelf below mine. The entire section erupted with shouts of support.

"See you!" EnvyFree yelled.

I sank into Stubby's warm coat pocket, nestled beside a thick roll of cash, a wad of concert tickets I knew he didn't have the license to sell, and questionable strands of diamond jewellery. "Oh, Stubbs, my man. Looks like you've been a busy boy. Here we go again."

Stretching my stiff pages and flexing my covers, I prepared for some serious reading sessions. *This is going to be great.*

But as he started walking, instead of vibrating with eagerness, I found myself contemplating the future. What if one of these times, Stubby really *was* successful in his quest and didn't need me anymore? He'd live the life his grandmother wished for him. He'd be happy...

A sudden panic swelled, seeping into my binding. That wouldn't actually happen though, right? I couldn't fathom losing him.

"Wait—what am I thinking? I'm a self-help book. That's the whole reason I exist," I muttered. Helping Stubby heal should be my top priority. *Then why isn't it?*

Realization thumped like an encyclopedia dropped on the floor. Truth was, I needed the guy...like, truly *needed* him. Craved him. All this time, I'd been selfishly relying on his repeated failure so he'd read me again. Almost like an addict. My pages tingled, and I quickly scanned through my own material. A heavy sigh followed.

No, not *almost.*

I gave my spine a firm shake. "Get your fonts on straight, Rewire. No more of this nonsense. You gotta practice what you preach."

Freshly bolstered in my passion to help, not to mention kick my habit, I willed Stubby to dig his heels in and really commit to change. If he started strong today, he stood a solid chance of recovery. *This* could be the time he succeeded.

I felt our momentum shift as Stubby stopped to talk to someone. Nimble fingers reached past me inside the pocket to pull out a couple of tickets. Before his jacket closed again, I caught a glimpse of the dusty drapes framing the library window.

"Excuse me. You two look like music lovers," Stubby said. His voice was muffled, but I could still make it out. "Listen, my sister died recently, and we were supposed to go to this concert together. I just *can't* bring myself to go now, but I know she would've hated to see these go to waste. To honour her memory, I'm letting them go for a very reasonable price..."

To honour her memory? Really?

Stubby didn't have a sister. So much for that strong start. The guy hadn't even made it out of the library.

Groaning, I dog-eared pages he'd need to read first once he finally opened me. "Well... maybe next time, buddy."

But then I smiled. *Next time.*

DON'T POP 'TILL YOU GET ENOUGH

Charlie was a guy who typically kept to himself. He was a little on the chunky side and a bit nerdy. At least, that's what everyone made fun of him for. This was the very first dance Charlie had ever been to, and he was probably the biggest wallflower in the room.

The dance started quite uneventfully. The girls and boys lined the walls opposite one another, everyone eyeing each other up and feeling awkward. The air was filled with heavily doused cologne and pubescent angst. Charlie tugged on the snug dress shirt he wore. He'd clearly gained a few pounds since his aunt's wedding last summer, but desperate to look presentable, he wore it anyway. Normally he didn't care about this kind of stuff. However, tonight was different. Charlie only came because of *her*.

Cindy... He snuck a longing glance in her direction as he went to get a drink. She was the prettiest girl in school. And smart, too! She had won the spelling bee this year. Her curly brown hair was pulled back into a cascading ponytail of ringlets. Looking into her eyes was like seeing all the green of summer at the same time. And he couldn't forget the cute splash of freckles across her cheeks, which always made his heart skip. Charlie watched her pink dress sway around her legs as she moved absent-mindedly to the music.

Cindy's eyes scanned around the room, keen in their observation, and landed directly on his. Charlie quickly looked away and chugged his punch, feeling caught in the act. He tried desperately to look cool.

"Hi, Charlie," soon came the voice of an angel.

His eyes grew wide for a split second as he looked over to see Cindy standing there. He had been so lost in thought, or panic rather, that he didn't notice her approach. *She spoke to me...* Gulping down his nerves, Charlie couldn't manage to force a word out. His throat felt drier than a popcorn fart, so he simply smiled instead.

"It's good to see more people are dancing... *Finally.*" She laughed shyly, pouring some punch into a glass. Her delicate braces glinted beneath the swirling disco ball lights.

"No kidding. Way more!" he answered, far too enthusiastically. *Reel it in, stupid.*

They smiled at each other, silence overtaking them. Charlie nervously clicked his heels, furiously contemplating. *Should I? What better time than now?*

"So, Cindy," he ran a clammy hand through his wavy hair. "Would you, uh... like to dance?"

"Sure."

Holy shit.

They walked out onto the crowded dance floor, stealing furtive glances. Charlie discretely checked his breath and popped in a piece of gum. He noticed how easily Cindy moved to the upbeat song. Charlie swayed stiffly at first but found he felt more comfortable as the melody bopped along.

As his confidence grew, so did his moves. He executed a quick spin with a flourish and thought, *I'm actually pretty good at this dancing thing.* His smile grew wider. Getting carried away, Charlie decided to emulate something he'd seen in a Michael Jackson video once, but his toe caught on his shoe. Much to his dismay, he lost his footing. As his torso lurched backward and his arms swung wide, his already snug shirt stretched even further. Suddenly, a button popped off with great force... and hit Cindy right in the eye.

A look of wide-eyed shock crossed her face a split second before she turned away, grabbing to cover it. Unfortunately, the kids around them just had to see what happened and started to laugh, fingers pointing.

Charlie didn't know what to do. Mortified, he panicked and muttered a stuttering, "I'm sorry," before making a bee-line toward the gym doors. He just wanted to shrink into absolute nothingness and disappear. Sliding to a stop around a corner down the hall, he buried his face in his hands.

Charlie could only imagine how red his cheeks were in that moment. A mental image of Cindy's eye popped out of its socket flitted through his mind, and he slammed his palms down on the ground. *Stupid, stupid, stupid!* He'd kick himself if he could. *I just ruined any slim chance I might have had with her.*

He hoped she was okay. He should probably man-up and go back in there to check on her, but he couldn't muster up the nerve just yet.

Suddenly, Charlie heard footsteps approaching briskly down the hall. He cringed and flattened against the wall, trying to stay as invisible as he wished he was.

A pair of pink shoes appeared on the shiny waxed hallway before him, coming to a stop with a click. He recognized those shoes. Surprised, Charlie looked up to see Cindy standing there. The light emanating from a nearby window framed her in a most brilliant silhouette. He could tell her eye was definitely a touch on the red side, yet she was smiling. The breath caught in his throat.

She held her hand out toward him, her smile growing larger. Simultaneously feeling curious and confused, Charlie pushed himself up to his feet. He looked down at her open palm.

She was holding out a button.

His button.

DATE NIGHT

"Two minutes and ten seconds." I tossed a plastic-wrapped popcorn packet across the kitchen. Cathy snagged it out of the air with one hand, pinching at the plastic ends to tear it open.

"Yeah, yeah, I got it under control," she muttered with a wry grin, waving me away. "You just get the movie ready."

Raising my hands in surrender, I laughed as I meandered into the adjoining living room.

Popping in a cheesy-looking romantic comedy—it was date night, after all—I paused to glance past the partial wall into the kitchen. A Latin-flavoured song played on the radio, inspiring my girlfriend's voluptuous hips to sway to the beat. Her eyes closed as she savoured the music, and I could not keep from smiling.

Crouching low, I padded in her direction, carefully sneaking up from behind in my socked feet. The corn popped in the microwave; the smell made my mouth water. I hid behind the table as Cathy did a spin before falling back into step, knowing exactly what she was doing.

A moment later she spun again, but this time, she crashed right into me.

Her eyes popped open in surprise and a squeak escaped her lips.

Laughing, my arms circled her waist, pulling her in close. I found one of her hands and held it tucked into the nook of my shoulder.

"You scared the crap out of me, Dale," Cathy whispered fervently before joining in with a laugh of her own. She allowed me to lead her in a sloppy salsa step, nodding in approval.

"Not bad, hey?" I raised an arm and spun her around, then reeled her back in. The movement felt nostalgic, reminiscent of how we first met at a Cinco de Mayo party a buddy dragged me to years ago. This dark-haired beauty took pity on me, striking up conversation at the food table. It didn't take long for her chocolate eyes to captivate me, and I asked her to dance. I must've stomped on her feet in just the right way because here we were.

"I'm impressed. You've been practicing."

Wiggling my eyebrows up and down, a mischievous grin crossed my face. "I've been learning from an exceptional teacher. Beautiful, smart, and sexy. You know, they say Latin dancing can be quite the aphrodisiac." As if she didn't know.

Our eyes locked, smoldering as our hips moved together to the rhythm. Like magnets, our lips gravitated toward each other, touching just as the back door swung open and banged against the wall.

Immediately stilling, we dropped our hands and stepped back with a chuckle. Not that it mattered if my daughter saw us kiss, as Cathy and I had been dating for quite some time now, but I still preferred not to wave the fact that her mother and I weren't together anymore in her face. Lucky for me, Sam seemed to be one of the rare kids who actually *liked* her father's girlfriend.

"Hi, Dad! Hi, Cathy. Me and my friend Erin will be downstairs playing video games, okay?" Sam whirled through the back foyer like a tornado, followed by the sound of boots clattering and jackets falling to the floor. Seconds later, two pairs of feet thudded down the stairs.

I zipped around the corner into the foyer and called down the stairs, "Hey, hang your coats, please! We weren't born in a barn, were we?"

The footsteps froze at the bottom of the stairwell, then Sam jogged back up, reappearing on the landing. The freckles peppering her cheeks moved as she flashed me a smile. Her auburn hair was pulled up into some kind of curly pigtails that reminded me of her first-grade school photo. Funny how fads repeated themselves. She'd been so little, such an enormous difference compared to the sixteen-year-old version standing before me. I couldn't believe how much my little girl had grown up. Time was moving too fast.

Resisting the moisture building behind my eyes, I asked, "How was play rehearsal?"

Sam shrugged. "Good, I guess. Same old." Scooping up the coats, she shoved them onto the hooks on the wall.

"Do you guys want some popcorn?"

"Not right now, thanks! Maybe later." Then, with a hurried wave, Sam bounded down the stairs again.

I sighed, returning to the kitchen.

Cathy stood holding a bowl of buttery popcorn, a sympathetic smile on her face. She knew how hard it was on me to watch my daughter grow up, needing her father less and less. She'd felt similar feelings, having practically raised her baby sister after their mother passed tragically at a young age. She'd confided that stepping back to let her sister leave the nest and learn to fly had been challenging, but necessary—and eventually, rewarding.

"Movie time?" she asked, motioning toward the couch.

Smiling back, I nodded. "Let's do it."

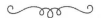

THE MOVIE WAS WORSE THAN I IMAGINED IT WOULD BE. Overly sappy, unrealistic, and bad acting. Almost as bad as those damn *Hallmark* Christmas movies I always got forced to watch. My votes to watch *Die Hard* or *Christmas Vacation* had been vetoed by Sam and Cathy two years running now—ever since Cathy started spending more time here. Sometimes it really sucked being the lone man in the equation. Perhaps someday, whenever Sam got married, I'd finally have some backup.

Whoa, pump the brakes. I extinguished that thought from my brain as fast as it flickered; marriage was a long way off for my baby girl.

I didn't even want to consider that yet.

Lucky for me, nature offered a perfectly timed distraction. "I gotta go drain the main vein," I announced with a grin, disengaging myself from Cathy's arms.

"Good luck," she quipped as I stood with a groaning stretch.

Laughing, I walked down the hall and slipped out of view. The bathroom was quiet, save for the muffled sounds of video game action sequences blaring through the floor vent. As I did my business, the odd shout, giggle, or squeal rose. *Must be a good video game.*

Washing my hands, I noticed something different from the corner of my eye. Above the toilet on the cabinet's open bottom shelf, I spied a velvety slip case. Curious, I investigated. It was feather light and rattled when I shook it. "What are you?"

I opened the top, and a slender package slid out easily. Realization dawned as I recognized the tiny two-toned pills arranged in perfect rows. I'd never seen a package exactly like this one before, but I *had* seen similar packages throughout the entirety of my first marriage. Why had Cathy left them sitting there? Was it just by mistake? Or...

I walked back into the living room, reclaiming my spot on the couch and assuming the cuddle position once more. I kissed the top of her forehead. "I saw what you left in the bathroom..." I whispered, chuckling awkwardly. "Are you trying to tell me something?"

Cathy craned her neck to look at me, a bewildered look in her eye. "What are you talking about?"

Squeezing her shoulder supportively, I continued, "Listen, I know we've been together for a few years now, and I agree—it would be amazing to live together—but I still worry about what Sam will feel, ya know?"

Cathy's bewilderment turned to confusion, her eyebrows raising with a headshake. "What? I mean, *yes,* I'd love to live together...but *what?*" She sat up, twisting in my arms.

It was my turn to be confused. "Okay, so you just left them there by accident then?"

"Left what, where?"

"Your pill package—you know, *the pill.* In the bathroom." I pointed a thumb in the hallway's direction. "Honestly, it's not a big deal if you want to leave some here."

Cathy's eyes widened; lips pursed. Tucking her hair behind her ears, she stood.

"What's going on right now? What's up?" I prodded, standing with her.

She shook her head vigorously, then pushed my chest back down with her hand. "No, no, you should definitely stay sitting."

I resettled onto the couch but leaned forward, watching her pace away, then back again. She seemed to be struggling to find words, and I raised my brows, losing patience. "Are you going to tell me or what?" I crossed my arms over my chest in one fluid motion.

Cathy paused beside the couch, then gently sat down beside me, perching tentatively, ready to move as though she were defusing a bomb that could explode any minute. Placing a hand on my shoulder, she looked me squarely in the eye. Her words came slowly, deliberately. "Don't freak out...but those aren't my pills."

"Not your pills? But then who—" I froze, a chill running the length of my body. My eyes darted toward the basement stairs, then back again as I inhaled a huge gulp of air. "No." I shot up from the couch, slicing a hand through the air.

Cathy nodded. "Yes."

"No," I repeated more firmly, running my fingers through my thinning hairline. "That's not possible; she's only sixteen." My hands felt clammy. The collar tightened like a noose around my neck. *The pill.*

"Hun, I had sex for the first time when I was sixteen—not that I'm proud of that fact. Sadly, it's not an uncommon occurrence. At least she's being safe! That's something to be happy abou—"

"I should be *happy* my daughter is sexually active?" I walked a circle around the couch, unable to stay still and uncertain what to do with my hands. They went from my hair to my neck, then into my pockets before finally being shoved beneath my armpits.

"Well, no, I didn't mean it like that—"

"Then how did you mean it?" I blurted, arms thrusting into the air. "I can't do this right now," I muttered, shaking my head. Turning away, I stalked down the hall. The bathroom door slammed closed with me leaning against it.

No, this can't be.

My gaze fell onto the pills right away, my body reacting as if the package might jump out and bite me. My heart rate spiked, the ol' ticker slamming inside my chest at an ever-increasing speed. I ripped my gaze away from the pills to stare into the mirror, wiping the beaded sweat from my brow. My worst nightmare had come true.

"My little girl," I moaned, collapsing forward. Burying my head in my hands, elbows resting on the countertop, a tear slipped down my cheek. "My baby..."

I wasn't ready for this.

Everywhere I looked, all I could see were those pills. They were multiplying, taunting me, terrorizing. I finally had to snatch them off the shelf and shove the velvety case inside the cupboard. I hoped that hiding them from view might help ease the turmoil grinding inside me, but I still felt just as horrified.

This was even worse than the great tampon discovery of 2018.

Images flashed through my mind, a barrage of missiles exploding into my consciousness. A slideshow of Sam's life. I saw her grow from a babbling infant into a rough-and-tumble toddler. After that came the adorable grade-schooler stage before she morphed into a surprisingly snotty pre-teen, which finally brought me to the fearless teenager she was now.

That's when the unwanted images started. I stared into the mirror with wide-eyed horror as, right before my eyes, Sam held the pill package. After popping one into her mouth, she giggled with glee and pulled a shaggy-haired pubescent boy in to suck on her lips. I tried to blink the vision away but couldn't. When the boy pulled a condom out of his pocket, I growled like the true papa-bear

I was, pushing away from the vanity. Grasping to relieve the anger boiling inside me, I wrapped my fingers around the shower curtain and yanked with all my strength, sending the curtain and rod crashing down. My breath came hard and fast as I let loose a guttural shout.

A knock sounded at the door.

"Dale, honey? Are you okay in there?" came Cathy's concerned voice.

I stilled—caught, realizing what I'd just done.

"I'm fine," I called back.

"It doesn't sound very fine. It *will* be okay, you know. You remember what it was like to be a teenager, don't you?"

My eyes opened so wide, they felt like they'd merged with my eyebrows. I remembered exactly what I was like at that age. A hormonal teenage boy obsessed with girls.

The memory of Sam in the foyer suddenly resurfaced. She'd hung up their jackets, both hers and her friend Erin's. My mind zeroed in on the jackets like a pair of telescopic binoculars. Sam had squashed her furry-collared purple coat on top of a blue and green ski-doo jacket. No sixteen-year-old girl I'd ever seen Sam hang out with wore a ski-doo jacket.

Could Erin actually be Aaron?

An idea dawned, its light flashing upon me brighter than a solar flare. Feeling a mighty rush of energy, I swung the bathroom door open and breezed past a very perplexed Cathy. Trudging with purposeful steps, I disappeared into my bedroom to retrieve precisely what I'd need to rectify this situation. Cathy barely made it to the doorway before I breezed past her again, heading in the opposite direction.

She gave chase down the hall. "Um, what's with the bat?"

"I'm going to make sure my daughter stays *un*-sexually active."

Cathy shook her head, trying to get ahead of me as I strode through the living room into the kitchen. Worry filled her face. "I'm sorry, and how can you do that with a bat?"

She grabbed my arm to stop me, but I pulled away, jogging down the small set of stairs into the backdoor foyer. I yanked Sam's coat off the hook, revealing the ski-doo jacket beneath. "Does that look like a girl's coat to you?" I took it off the hook and inspected it. I smelled it, looking at Cathy with a triumphant grin. "That's cologne."

I tossed the coat, gripping the bat handle a little tighter. *That kid's going to get it.* After today, word would spread and every single boy for miles around would know that Sam was off limits.

"Okay, not only is our date night ruined, but you're also starting to scare me. Are you saying there's a *boy* in the basement right now?" Cathy scoffed, leaning against the wall. "C'mon, Sam's not that stupid. When a boy picked her up for her very first dance, you answered the door sharpening your hunting knife."

I smirked, remembering the blissfully horrified look on that kid's face.

Cathy met me on the landing, placing her hands on my chest. "You need to calm down. I know you're concerned—I get that—but *all* kids have to grow up sometime, and we just need to roll with it. I want you to take some deep breaths with me." She inhaled purposefully.

Looking between Cathy and the basement, I felt torn. Somewhere deep down I knew she was right. The rational part of my brain suggested that regardless of how awkward or hard it might be, sitting down and having a calm talk with my daughter was the best thing to do. Unfortunately, the irrational part of my brain was all hyped up on adrenaline, and logic wasn't exactly landing on all fours.

"I'll breathe later," I mumbled, jogging down the stairs.

"Dale," she whisper-shouted as she followed. "Dale!"

I half expected to find this boy lying on top of my little Sam as I rounded the corner at the bottom of the stairs leading into the rec room. *Playing video games, my ass. This kid will learn the hard way how to keep his hands to himself.*

"Dale, stop!"

"Oh, I'm not going to hurt him...much." I grinned devilishly.

The lights were off as we entered the room, a flickering television screen providing the only illumination. I caught sight of the boy on the couch right away. Yep, it was most definitely a boy, leaning back against the cushions. A growl rumbled in my throat.

My eyes strained in the low light, struggling to see Sam. I quickly realized she wasn't sitting beside the boy at all. No, not beside. She was kneeling in front of him, her head bent as she leaned over him. I heard Cathy's gasp beside me. White-hot rage surged like lightning, an unbridled energy coursing through my veins. Fiery fury exploded from every pore, consumed my mind, and burned a hole through whatever patience I might have possessed.

"That's enough!" I roared like a beast on the rampage. Spinning my bat between my hands, I surged forward to break up this new nightmare.

Sam's eyes snapped up from her task, completely horrified. "Dad, no!" The boy she'd been leaning over squealed and cringed, curling his legs up into a ball on the couch. I reached out to grab him by the collar, but Sam threw her body in front of him, acting as a human shield.

"Move, Sam. This kid has worn out his welcome." She didn't budge, so I tossed my bat onto the adjacent chair and hooked my arms under her armpits. Hoisting her up, I swivelled and swiftly relocated my daughter behind me. Cathy was there to deal with Sam, so I turned my attention back to the couch. Taking hold of my bat again, I loomed over the so-called boy.

He avoided my eyes, his arms wrapped around his bent knees. I nudged his leg with the business end of my bat. "Get up," I ordered.

"Why are you doing this, Dad?" Sam shrieked.

"You left your pills upstairs. I know what you've been up to!" I shouted back.

"Dale," Cathy warned.

"I got this." I nodded, waving her off with a hand. Gritting my teeth and sharpening my focus, I reminded myself I couldn't actually hurt the kid. Cathy grumbled behind me, clearly not impressed with being dismissed so flippantly. I'd pay for that later.

"My pills? Is that what this is all about?" Sam stomped her foot defiantly. "Mom helped me get them. It's fine, Dad."

"Your *mother* helped you get them?" I was livid. How could

Janice do such a thing without consulting me? This was a big deal. Here I thought we respected each other more than that, but I guess I was wrong. A very long and angry discussion was imminent in our future.

"Yeah." Sam shrugged, then looked to her friend. "I'm so sorry, Aaron."

My steely gaze locked with my daughter's defiant one. Fuming, I rasped, "So, your mother knows you're having *sex*?"

Sam's brows shot up; her hands raised. "Wait—no, I'm not having sex."

I scoffed. "Yeah right, okay. Nobody goes on the pill unless they're having sex. Or planning on it."

"That's not true!"

I ignored her feeble attempt at a denial, turning back to the boy. "Now you, get up!"

"Sir, I didn't do anything wrong," the boy snivelled, frozen in place.

"I'll be the judge of that. You think you can take advantage of my daughter and get away with it? Get up! I won't say it again," I shouted, holding the bat aloft. Cathy just stood and shook her head. She'd planted her hands firmly on her hips, quietly letting the scene play out. I was a little irritated that she wasn't helping more.

At the sight of my raised bat glowing in the television's light, the boy struggled to his feet, stumbling then righting himself again. *Is he drunk?* Trembling, he glanced between me, Sam, and the stairs.

"I swear, I never touched her."

"Stop it, Dad! There was nothing sexual going on!" Sam bellowed, breaking away from Cathy to intercede again. Holding her hands up, her eyes were as incredulous as they were wide. Cathy slipped away to turn the lights on, and within seconds, illumination washed the basement with a much-needed clarity.

I paused, looking between my daughter and Aaron, suddenly noticing that their hair wasn't ruffled, nor was their clothing dishevelled. Aaron's pants weren't open or down—no surprises hanging out. And at that moment, I also observed a thick walking cast on his leg. The thick casing was covered in scribbles and drawings, its original white colour nearly gone. *Well, that explains his stumbling.*

"Wait...so, you weren't just doing what I thought you were doing?"

"What did you think I was doing?" Sam snapped back, grabbing the pack of markers off the nearby coffee table. She brandished them like a weapon. "I was drawing on Aaron's cast."

"Drawing? Oh, thank goodness." My head lolled back on my shoulders, bat drooping. The relief I felt was palpable. Okay, so that was one disaster successfully averted, but more questions needed answers. "That still doesn't explain the pills, young lady. Have you been having sex with this boy?"

Sam groaned, exasperated. "No!"

Aaron looked mortified. "Um sir?" he piped up. "I'm gay."

I blinked, then set the bat down.

"He's one of my friends from Drama Club," Sam explained, tossing the markers back down onto the coffee table. "At least he *was* my friend. Probably not anymore after today." With an apologetic look on her face, she looked to Aaron again. The boy returned a nervous smile.

"Thank you for telling us the truth, Sam. That's wonderful," Cathy chimed in, sending out encouraging and calming vibes with her voice. "And it's nice to meet you, Aaron." Her demeanour was kind and motherly. She'd always been good with my daughter, one of the many reasons I loved her. Sam returned Cathy's smile, before retraining an icy scowl on me.

My brain hurts. I sliced my hands through the air. "Well then, who are you sleeping with?"

"Nobody!" everyone in the room answered at once.

It was my turn to plant my hands on my hips, utterly confused. "Okay, will somebody just explain then, cause I'm getting sick of asking questions."

Cathy walked up beside me and calmly put her arm around my waist, an understanding smile on her lips.

Sam rolled her eyes to the ceiling tiles. "Are you actually going to listen?"

Cathy gave my side a squeeze, and I nodded solemnly. "I will."

After pushing out a heavy breath of air, she answered, "Fine. I got the pill for my acne, okay? It's supposed to help clear it up."

Acne. Who knew?

Aaron's eyes lit up as he ran a hand over his own somewhat pimply face. "Oh, really? I didn't know about that. Does that work for guys, too?"

Sam shrugged. "I don't know. I doubt it because I think it's all hormone based. It's made up of...oh, crap, what do they call it?"

"Estrogen," Cathy offered.

She smiled. "Yeah! That's it. Estrogen, the super girly hormone. I don't think you'd want that in your body." Sam looked back at her friend, scrunching her nose.

"Or would I?" Aaron laughed, pretending to flick some imaginary hair over his shoulder.

Sam giggled, and the two began chattering amongst themselves, completely ignoring the adults still standing in the room. Every so often Sam shot glares my way, and I knew it would be a long while before I lived this one down. *I guess I have some serious 'making up' to do.*

I looked down to see Cathy staring up at me with a mirthful grin.

"What else was a guy supposed to think?" I whispered, shrugging. She'd gasped too when we first saw them on the couch. "So, sue me for being an overprotective parent."

In response, Cathy simply smiled and stretched up to kiss me on the cheek. That was her silent signal for 'we'll talk about it later.' Or maybe it was 'there's a lesson in this for you'. Either one seemed applicable. Next, she motioned towards the kids with a head tilt.

Groaning inwardly, I swallowed my bruised pride. "Hey, kids... look, I'm sorry for the confusion. Sorry to you, Sam, for getting my wires crossed. And for scaring you too, Aaron. I hope you'll accept my apology...oh, and Aaron, if you *didn't* want to tell your parents what happened, I'd be okay with that."

I received unimpressed looks in return.

More than ready to leave the room, I advised Sam that Aaron

would have to go home soon, then collected my bat and turned toward the stairs. Shaking my head, I ascended, feeling utterly exhausted. This was a new era and I clearly had to get up to speed.

Cathy fell into step beside me, sharing an approving nod. "Good apology. We can still salvage our date night—you know, now that all the excitement has passed. Wanna go finish our movie?"

I flashed the biggest smile I could muster, and took her hand into mine. "Forget the movie. I need a drink."

MOMENTS TO CHERISH

C arrie put on her scratched and weather-worn leather slippers, their navy shade faded from many adventures into the backyard, and crossed the kitchen towards the garden doors.

She walked out onto the screen porch and settled into her puffy chair for the first time that day—which happened to be near midnight. It was often the only time she managed to claw back for herself.

Her hair was a dishevelled mess, and her eyes showcased a bleary shade of bloodshot, but she was ready to work. Propping her exhausted feet up on the wicker coffee table, Carrie pulled out her shiny, silver pen. Her favourite.

Her ink-stained fingers set to work. Running skilled strokes across the page, they methodically shaped seemingly haphazard markings into recognizable form. First some chubby cheeks, then big button eyes, followed by two stubby legs. Finally, she completed her character creation with a cute, puffy diaper.

An odd shadow flitted across the deck boards, immediately catching her attention. Carrie's eyes darted toward the garden door, searching beyond the glass barrier into the house. However, nothing out of the ordinary presented itself. No movement at all. She looked up at the strings of patio lanterns dangling above. Perhaps a big moth was to blame, flying past a light.

Carrie had just lowered her eyes back to her sketchbook when another shadowy blip registered in her peripheral vision. *That's no moth.* Like a hawk seeking prey, her eyes snapped back to the door, scanning what was visible of the dining and living room. She waited more patiently this time. But still there was nothing.

Hmm... Carrie knew it couldn't be her husband, Matthew; he slept like he was six feet under. She could practically feel his snores reverberating through the exterior wall. But it wasn't entirely impossible that he'd gotten up. Skeptical, she lowered her eyes back to the page, pushing hard to complete the very last illustration for her first picture book. Despite feeling like a zombie, the sheer excitement of completing a project stirred her last remnants of energy.

A distinctive cry sliced through the peaceful night air, the sound shrill, piercing. A child's squeal. Carrie jolted into immediate action, whipping the garden door open and running back inside the house. Flying into the baby's room first, she was relieved to see a sleeping lump of cuteness nestled in the crib, sweetly cuddling his bedtime blankie.

Carrie shifted to her toddler's bedroom next. Empty. *Ah ha.* A distinct sensation of déjà-vu seeped into her being. Cursing the day that child had ever learned to turn a doorknob, she carried onward. The hunt was on for her little mischief maker.

Carrie walked through the living room. A simultaneously sweet and pungent aroma wafted in the air, infiltrating her senses. The new Scentsy fragrance she'd tried today still lingered in the air—an instant favourite. However, an unpleasant odour mixed in with it, marring the previously pleasing scent. Something distinctive and instantly recognizable. Carrie's heart sank, shoulders slumping as she let out a frustrated sigh.

She rounded the corner, spying nothing amiss in the kitchen. *Slap, slap.* Sickly wet smacking sounds called out to her from the foyer. Carrie approached with dread. The aroma assaulted her nose more intensely with each step. Taking a deep breath, she glanced around the partition wall leading to the rear entrance.

"Mommy!"

"Oh, for the love of—"

She lowered to one knee. "What have you done?"

Little Eithan stood beside the door smacking his hands against the white painted surface, his fingers and palms thoroughly coated with the soft mush of poop. Smeared drawings of smiley faces, houses, and letters in the alphabet adorned his chosen canvas. What's worse, Eithan's face and chest had also been liberally decorated with the same nutty brown.

Well, it looks like I won't be finishing my project tonight.

Carrie recoiled as Eithan suddenly came in for a big hug. She grabbed his little arms and held him at bay, unable to avoid touching some of the offending substance.

"Where is your diaper sweetie?"

Her mind swirled as it formulated a plan of attack, none of which involved remaining poop-free. Finally, after taking a deep breath, she bit the bullet and picked him up. She certainly didn't want him walking through the house like this. Besides, clothes could be washed.

Another shriek pierced the air. This time, a guttural baritone.

Carrie converged upon the source as she carried Eithan toward the bathroom. Her husband—bless his soul—had found the missing diaper, its leftovers now cold and greasy. He stared with mouth agape, then pointed in horror at the raw carnage distributed so skillfully around the little room. The back door was just a tease. Here lay the toddler's true masterpiece.

Matthew glanced at Carrie standing in the doorway, then promptly did a double-take. He swung his pointer finger toward little Eithan and cried out with fresh terror.

Carrie stifled a laugh at his reaction.

"Oh good, you're up."

FOR KING AND COOKIES

"How dare you steal cookies from the king!" Sir Maggins bellowed, thrusting a sword toward the thief.

The sticky-fingered culprit, Raya Hood, turned from the table of delicacies, quickly shoving a cookie in her mouth. Caught and now desperate for a weapon, she yanked a golden candlestick off the table and brandished it. "Don't come any closer!"

Sir Maggins chortled. "You think you can beat me with *that*? Raya Hood, if you give up now, I won't make you walk the plank!"

Raya Hood crunched on the stolen cookie. "Um...the plank?"

The knight bristled. "Yes, the plank! All the best castles have planks." Sir Maggins stomped haughtily. "Do you give up?"

The thief tapped her chin, thinking, before throwing the candlestick at the knight, who jumped out of the way. That momentary distraction provided the perfect opening. Raya Hood dashed past Sir Maggins, shouting, "I'll never surrender to your evil king!"

The knight roared, giving chase.

Raya Hood fled down hallway after hallway. So many hallways! Sir Maggins' armour clinked and clanked close behind. The rivals barrelled into a large hall littered with royal portraits. Bounding over a table, the thief targeted a heavy wooden door at the far end of the room. She tried to shove it closed behind her, but the knight blocked it with a metal-clad arm.

A huge spiral staircase lay before Raya Hood. Without a second thought, she bounded down the steps. "You'll never catch me!"

Sir Maggins pushed the door open with a grunt and sprinted after her foe. "Oh, yes, I will!"

Meanwhile, back on the patio...

Maureen sat down beside Tanis, handing her friend a glass of white wine. "Oh, my goodness. Look how nicely the kids are playing together. Isn't that adorable?"

"Absolutely," Tanis agreed, clinking her glass against Maureen's. "Such wild imaginations, these two. Usually, I have to chase Raya around like that—like, all the time." Tanis ran a hand through her platinum hair. "I love that child, but gosh, it's nice to get a break and just relax for a bit."

Maureen nodded enthusiastically. "Isn't that the truth?" She watched her own daughter Maggie chase after Raya, the two running round and around in tight circles. "What's happening now?"

Tanis smirked. "They're *obviously* running down a staircase."

Maureen chuckled, sipping her wine. "I wish I had that kind of energy."

"Oh, God, I know. I consider getting out of bed each morning an achievement."

Back in the kingdom...

Slightly dizzy, Raya Hood dashed out the castle keep. She whistled. Seconds later, her trusty steed—a black stallion named Bubbles —galloped to her rescue. Leaping off the steps, the clever thief landed on her horse's back and pumped a fist. "Ha ha! You'll never get me now!"

"You wanna bet?" Sir Maggins couldn't whistle, so she cock-a-doodle-doo'd instead. Her horse—a pretty white one named Sprinkles—heard the call and flew around the corner, skidding to a halt.

She promptly jumped into the saddle and took off after the thief. *Again.*

Hooves pounded and wind whipped as the pair galloped toward the castle exit.

"Raise the drawbridge!" Sir Maggins screamed at the top of her lungs. Steel chains clinked as soldiers cranked the rusty handles of two large reels controlling the bridge. "Hurry!"

Raya Hood kicked her heels, urging her horse to go faster. "C'mon, Bubbles! We need to get across!" She was close now, but the bridge was rising fast. After passing beneath a thick stone archway, her mount's hooves thundered up the drawbridge as it lifted. "C'mon!"

"Raise it! Hurry!" Sir Maggins cried, stopping Sprinkles at the base of the now angular bridge. A sludgy moat filled with snapping crocodiles lay below. Only a fool would try to jump across *that*.

The bridge was raised halfway now. She watched as Raya Hood's horse scrambled to climb. It was only a matter of time.

"Wuuaaaahhh!" Raya Hood wailed as Bubbles slipped and slid backwards. "Oh, no!" Bubbles neighed as they skidded down the planks to land at the bottom with a *thunk*.

Back on the patio...

"When will the treehouse be finished?" Maureen asked Tanis.

"Soon. Raya keeps trying to play on it. I have to watch her like a hawk. It really should've been done last weekend, but Mike got called to work *again*. He's been working so much lately—late hours. Then he's tired and grumpy whenever he is home." She shook her head, lips pursed.

Maureen reached out to give her friend's hand a supportive squeeze. "I'm sure it'll pass soon. He'll get caught up with work, and things will go back to normal." As a doctor, she knew all about working long hours and being sapped of energy. Maureen presented a cheerful smile, trying to steer their conversation back to happier topics. "It'll be so nice when the treehouse is all done."

Tanis swallowed her last gulp of wine, then returned the smile. "It really will."

Vigorous action unfolding on the lawn stole Maureen's attention. She grabbed her phone and snapped a quick picture. "Aw, look at them riding their brooms—er, *horses*."

"So cute. Now if only we could get them to use those brooms around the house. Amiright?" Tanis raised her brows.

Maureen nodded. "Preach it, Mama. I dream of chore charts."

"Mom goals."

In the kingdom...

Sir Maggins pulled out her sword. "I've got you now, thief!"

"My. Name. Is. Raya Hood!" She yanked a sword from her saddle's sheath. "I warn you, *knight*—the best fighter in all the land trained me. Sir Brother of Homesley!"

Sir Maggins laughed. "Well, *Merlin* taught me himself! So there!" She lunged forward, thrusting her sword toward Raya Hood. The thief smacked it away, bounding sideways.

"Merlin? *Really*? Wow. Did he teach you magic too?" Raya Hood couldn't help but ask as she swung her sword again. She'd do anything to learn magic. And Merlin...well, he was the best.

The knight leaned back, barely avoiding getting sliced. "Not yet, but he will," Sir Maggins replied, whipping her blade as fast as she could. Their swords crashed between them, shaking as they locked in an X. The rivals grunted and groaned while they pushed to overpower each other.

On the patio...

"Guys, no sticks in the faces! You know better," Tanis warned, her pointer finger making wide circles in front of her nose. The children groaned but lowered their weapons to a safer level before continuing. Tanis muttered from the side of her mouth, "I'm betting at least two Band-Aids come out of this battle."

Maureen laughed, pulling a slightly crumpled box of bandages out of her purse. "One of the perks about being a doctor is having an unlimited supply. I came prepared."

In the kingdom...

Raya Hood sprinted towards the tower, dashing through the archway and up the rickety stairs. The tower swayed in the breeze, its stones old and crumbling. Her foot slipped on a step, and she squealed, grasping the wall.

"You've hit a dead end, Raya Hood! You've got nowhere to run. Now you're mine!" Sir Maggins cackled wildly, using her fingers to tickle the thief.

A peal of laughter escaped Raya Hood, but she managed to climb the last step. As she sprinted to the window, she shouted, "I have a magic rope, Knight. Now you can't follow me!"

Sir Maggins scowled; brows pinched. "I see I've underestimated you! But I won't make that mistake again!" She tried to steal the rope away. Their hands wrestled for ownership of the braided cord.

On the patio...

"Hey! What are you guys doing up there?" Tanis stood up, wagging a finger. "Raya, you know the treehouse isn't finished yet. Someone could fall and get hurt. Get down!"

"Now!" Maureen added.

"Okay..." the girls grumbled, then made their way back down the nailed wooden planks they'd climbed. Raya hit the ground first, crossing her arms with a sour face. But Maggie's foot snagged on a loose rung. Letting out a sharp yelp, she toppled several feet and landed with a *thunk*.

Maggie grabbed her knee and rolled to the side, crying.

Maureen rushed to her daughter's side, checking for damage. "Are you alright, sweetie?" The source of pain seemed to be Maggie's knee, and she settled her focus there. "What were you thinking? We said the tree house was *off-limits*."

Tanis hovered off to the side, wringing her hands. "I'm so sorry, Maureen. I should've roped it off or something."

Maureen shook her head. "It's not your fault, Tanis. This was more like a group mistake. The kids should've listened, and we should've been watching closer."

"It hurts!" Maggie wailed, pointing out the tiny cut on her kneecap—little more than a scratch.

"Don't worry. Dr. Mom to the rescue." Maureen retrieved her miracle cure from the deck. "You girls need to be more careful, okay?" She blew on the wound, then patched it with a Band-Aid. "There. All better."

"Thanks, Mommy," Maggie said with a sniff.

Maureen kissed her daughter's cheek. Then, smiling, her hands fumbled in the grass – an idea forming. She knew what might lift their spirits. "Psst...girls! Guess what? I've got a secret message for you."

Two sets of eyes widened, immediately curious.

"It's from the grand wizard, Merlin." Her fingers closed around two twigs. "I gave *him* a Band-Aid yesterday, and he asked me to give you these." She revealed the knotted sticks from behind her back. "They're magic wands! He said you're both very special wizards, and he'll teach you all about magic...if you want, that is."

Tanis shot her an approving grin.

Maggie and Raya hopped up and down, clamouring like baby birds at mealtime. Maureen winked back at her friend, fighting a smile, then handed each girl a twig.

Back in the kingdom...

"Look what I can do!" A shooting star exploded from Raya Hood's wand, and she squealed with delight. However, her smile quickly faded as a mysterious piece of paper fluttered down from the sky. Gasping, she snatched it out of mid-air.

"What is it?" Sir Maggins stopped growing flowers with her wand and ran over to see.

With wide eyes, the girls read the note. *"To my special wizards. Help, I've been kidnapped! Please save me! Merlin."*

They stared at each other. As if on cue, their lips curled. "Let's go!" They thrust out their wands, and in a flurry of flailing arms and legs, the wizards zoomed off on a new adventure.

On the patio...

Tanis bumped fists with Maureen. "Nice work out there. Wands. Merlin. *Genius.*"

"You want another glass of wine?"

"Hit me up."

RED NOSE AND A PARTY DRESS

"Laney, help!" I said with a frantic wave. My roommate sniffed the air, her eyes widening as she approached the kitchen counter. Taking in the flour-covered disaster I'd created; she cocked an eyebrow.

"Emily...whatcha doing?"

"Baking. Horribly." I donned oven mitts, saving a pan of helpless cupcakes from being scorched. Not burnt. *Success.*

"And why are you baking, exactly? You don't bake." She plucked a painfully flat cookie off a pile of failed experiments. She took a bite, her nose scrunching, then forced a smile. "Mmm..."

"Oh, please. They're horrendous."

"Yeah, perhaps a tad too much butter." She set the cookie down. "And salt."

"I know." I cringed. "Frick, I suck at baking. But I need to make something edible for Lizzie's birthday party tomorrow! You made yours already?"

Laney's brows shot up. "Say what now?"

"You know, for the party. Tina asked us to bring a dessert." Tina was the first of our friend trio to start a family, naming me and Laney surrogate aunts for little Lizzie. I took my duties very seriously. Being an only child – and perpetually cursed in relationships – Lizzie was likely the closest I'd ever get to having a baby of my own to cuddle. I didn't want to disappoint her by bringing sub-par food to the party.

"Oh." Laney pointed with a flourish. "My contribution is in the pantry."

I opened the door. "Subway cookies?"

She plopped onto a stool. "Why not? The kiddies will like them more than anything I could ever make."

Laney took in my expression—an equal measure of disbelief and bitter jealousy, then waved her hand across the mess. "Listen, I'll help you however I can before I leave for Gavin's. We'll slap a ton of icing on whatever tastes best. It'll be fine."

"Thank you." The words rushed from my lips. Then I quickly added, "And don't tell Jared I made them." At the party tomorrow, I was being set up with Gavin's friend from the gym—supposedly rich, hot, and newly single. "Men want women who can bake and stuff."

Laney let out a snort of laughter over my choice of verbiage, then levelled her gaze. "Not all men care about that. The good ones want a woman who's *adorable and real* – and that's *you* to a tee. Look, Jared agreed to come to a *kid's party* just to meet you. I'm sure it'll be fine."

"Yeah...we'll see." Fully armed with non-existent confidence, I doubted the match. But knowing they'd never let me off the hook, I decided it was worth a shot.

We set to work, and within the hour, my lumpy cupcakes had sprouted twisty pyramids of purple icing. I finished each one with sprinkle beads for eyes. "There. Now they're trolls. Lizzie loves that movie."

Laney nodded. "Yep, and icing makes anything taste good."

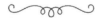

THE FOLLOWING DAY, I DISCREETLY SET MY CUPCAKES DOWN on the Disney-themed dining room table, hoping nobody saw. Seconds later, a small body crashed into my legs, the mini-version of Tina smiling up at me. I scooped Lizzie up into my arms, hugging her tight. "Happy birthday, my girl! How old are you today?"

"FOUR!" she shouted, beaming. Then she squirmed to get down, racing in a flurry of curly pigtails to join her friends in the living room. Balloons bopped back and forth, and squeals filled the already noisy space.

Laney and Tina waved me over. Wine in hand, I met them with one-armed hugs. "Wow, what a turnout."

"Yeah, most of Lizzie's class showed up!" Tina's bright smile tightened in the corners of her mouth; her brows pinched together ever so slightly as she worked to maintain an air of calm. "It's great but busy. Thanks for coming and for bringing snacks, guys. I think we'll need them."

"Can we help with anything else?" I asked.

"No, but thanks. The clown should be here soon. Then I can actually sit back and relax for a bit." Tina raised her wineglass in a toast. "To sanity." Our three glasses clinked together, meeting in the middle.

"You look gorgeous, by the way," Laney said, motioning to my form-hugging summer dress like Vanna White. I nodded in thanks, the praise making me feel special. I'd never been one to dress up often, as I much preferred the plaid shirt and rubber boot look I sported around my tiny—yet busy—vet clinic. It was a nice change of pace.

Laney tipped her chin towards a group of men chatting in the far corner. "Jared's been looking this way. He's the one between Gavin and Tim. In blue."

"Ah, I see..." My eyes casually slipped to the dark-haired GQ model. He had a sharp jawline, a perfectly windswept hairstyle, and chiselled muscles clearly visible beneath a snug collared shirt. "He's attractive." But would he be as good-looking on the inside?

"Just attractive?" Tina questioned, bewildered. "Quick reminder:

the man is a business owner, an Ivy League graduate, and has the body of a Greek God. Geez, I'd get hit by his lightning bolt any time." Finishing her wine, she smirked. "Don't tell Tim I said that."

"Our lips are sealed," Laney replied with a giggle while I turned an imaginary key to lock my mouth.

"Speaking of Tim." Tina flagged her husband down, giving him a silent signal to meet her in the kitchen. She turned back to us with an apologetic smile. "I need to go call the clown. He really should've been here by now. Good luck, Emily." Tina winked, then slipped out of the room.

Laney and I dove into planning how I should make contact. I preferred to wait for Jared to approach me—call me old-fashioned—but Laney insisted I be bold.

"Guys like assertive women. Besides, you're not the only single girl in the room." Laney pointed out two of Tina's PTA friends, eagerly scoping Jared out. "You need to take action."

"Right." As I pumped myself up, I took note of the fourth man standing in Jared's group. Tall and broad-shouldered, with tawny hair—slightly dishevelled, but well put together overall. "Who's the guy in green?"

Laney shrugged. "Huh? Oh, that's Cole—the heartthrob from Tina's PTA meetings."

"Oh...so *that's* Cole." I snuck another glance. From what Tina had told us, every single mom was after him. Poor guy lost his wife to cancer three years ago, now raising his daughter alone. I couldn't imagine how hard that must be.

Laney caught my admiring gaze, shaking her head. "Don't even bother, Em. Tina said he's off the market. The ungettable get. Not interested in dating."

My expression must've fallen because Laney snapped her fingers in my face. "Get your head in the game. Jared's a delicious slice of man pie, yours for the taking. Get over there."

"Right. Yes." I smoothed my dress. "No time like the present."

Just then, Tina and Tim returned to the living room, kneeling in front of Lizzie. The news couldn't have been good because the little girl who I loved to pieces started sniffling.

"Uh oh, what's going on?" Laney whispered.

Lizzie broke into tears, and my heart fell. They hugged her, but she pushed away to go hide in the corner. Tim went to comfort Lizzie as Tina faced the partygoers, announcing, "I've got some unfortunate news. It turns out the clown can't make it, but the party isn't over. Keep having fun! Birthday cake is coming soon."

Oh no, not the clown. Lizzie loves clowns.

Tina walked over, rubbing her neck. "Stupid clown said he double-booked. Dammit. Lizzie was so excited when we promised her a clown this year. It's literally all she wanted. I'm pissed."

"Asshole," Laney growled.

I looked over at Jared's chiselled face. He happened to glance my way, and we exchanged a smile. At the same time, I couldn't help but notice one of the attractive PTA moms inching her way closer to him. Laney was right; I had to get over there soon in order to stand a chance. But then I looked back at little Lizzie, currently crying on her father's shoulder. She was heartbroken.

Ah, crap...

I squared my shoulders, locking eyes with Tina. "Lizzie's getting a clown today."

My friend's eyes widened. "What?"

"I'll be the clown."

Laney set her glass down. "Do you even know how to be a clown?"

"Not at all, but I'll come up with something. A crappy clown is better than no clown." I looked between their stunned faces. "Right?"

As if on cue, the pair brightened, crushing me into a group hug. Tina clapped her hands. "Thank you, Em! Okay, upstairs now. We gotta dress you up."

As we rushed away, Tina paused to whisper in Tim's ear, and I slipped one last longing look at Jared. The woman stood right behind him now, stealing furtive glances. I sighed.

Oh, well. Lizzie is more important.

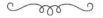

I TURNED FROM THE BATHROOM MIRROR, AGHAST. THE girls had teased, crimped, and sprayed my hair until it resembled a frizzy weeping willow. Halloween makeup slathered my skin, white overall, with green triangles above and below my eyes. Red lipstick ringed my mouth. I donned one of Lizzie's spongy clown noses, then tucked my dress into a pair of Tim's oversized pants. A baggy collared shirt, blazer, tie, and a sparkly child's tiara completed the look. My friends stepped back to admire their handiwork.

"It's perfect! She'll never know it's you," Tina chirped with glee.

"This is gonna be fun." Laney's grin was huge as she pulled us all together for a quick selfie.

Flapping my baggy arms, I giggled at the sheer ridiculousness of the situation. "See, this is why I don't go out much. Look what happens?" Giving a rueful shake of the head, I added, "Gosh, I'm actually nervous."

"Oh c'mon, you've done community theatre. You'll do great!" Laney rubbed my shoulders as though I were a boxer between rounds. "And getting out more is *good for you*."

Tina wiped moisture from her eye. "You're a lifesaver, Em. Truly, thank you."

I smiled, squeezing her hand. Then, pulling my shoulders back, I took one last look in the mirror. "Alright, alright. Let's just do this thing." With change jingling in one pocket and twisting balloons in the other, I snuck downstairs.

Tina strode into the living room and announced, "Glorious news, everyone! The clown could come after all. Lizzie, isn't that great? Sweety, sit right there and prepare to be entertained!"

After taking a deep breath, I jumped around the corner with jazz hands on full display. "Hello, kids! I'm Frizzy the Clown! Now, where's the birthday girl?"

Lizzie's eyes lit up like sparklers. "Me, me, me!" She thrust her hands up, bouncing.

Tim pulled the couch back, and parents wrangled their kids onto the area rug. Cole smiled as he sat down beside his adorable daughter. I had every child's rapt attention, which was perfect. The only person's interest I didn't seem to have, was Jared's. He wasn't looking at all, busy chatting with the woman I'd seen earlier. *Dammit.*

I shook it off, focusing on the task at hand.

Amidst cheers and laughter, I muddled my way through a haphazard clown act. I did cartwheels, tripped over my feet—a lot – and pretended I was descending an imaginary set of stairs. Lizzie loved it when I pulled a dime, a quarter, and finally a Looney out of her ear. Lucky for me, my sloppiness didn't seem to hinder the trick. Baffled, she snatched the coins from my hands, clinking them together.

Panic hit momentarily when I couldn't blow up the twisting balloons for my big finale. *Curse you, feeble lungs.* Thankfully, Tina and Laney jumped in to help. Cole, too, which was nice of him. Once every child had received a balloon sword—the only thing I could make—I swooped in to give Lizzie a birthday hug. Then, with one last cartwheel, I jazz-handsed my way out of there.

Mission complete.

TEN MINUTES LATER, I RETURNED TO THE PARTY. THERE had been no way to salvage the sweaty, spray-stiffened mess I once called hair. Laney gave it a valiant effort but just ended up pulling it into a tattered ponytail. My dress was damp from all my vigorous clowning, and though I'd scrubbed my face to within an inch of its life, faint outlines still remained. The remnants were visible to anyone who might look closely. Not like anybody would now.

With my throat parched and dignity hanging by a thread, I bee-lined it to the dining room for a drink. En route, I spied Jared speaking to a different woman now. He happened to glance my way, eyes roaming over my dishevelled form. On a whim, I flashed him what I believed to be a flirtatious smile. He'd agreed to come here to meet me after all. Maybe there was still a glimmer of a chance?

I got a tight-lipped, thanks-but-no-thanks smile in return. *Right. I guess that's that.* Oh well, it's not like the guy had made any effort to speak to me. It was a worthy sacrifice to make Lizzie smile. I poured a glass of berry punch and greedily gulped the ice-cold liquid.

"You still have a bit of clown on you."

The voice startled me, and I jumped, sending droplets of punch splattering on the floor. Turning, I saw Cole casually leaning against the doorway adjoining the dining room and kitchen.

"Sorry – what?"

Cole abandoned his position and approached with a smile. He pointed to the faint red ring that stained my mouth, his jade eyes twinkling. "Your clown makeup is still showing."

I chuckled nervously, trying to ignore the troll cupcake staring back at me from his plate. "Oh, yeah. Well, once a clown, always a clown, I guess." *Why did I just say that?* His steady gaze caught me off guard. Gosh, he was even cuter up close. *What am I thinking? He's the ungettable PTA dad, remember?*

Cole's smile grew. He leaned in. "I really admire what you did back there. You made Lizzie's day, and my daughter loved it, too. A new calling, perhaps?" He lifted the cupcake.

"Wow, thank you." I spied Tina and Laney pantomiming enthusiastic cheers from beyond Cole's view. Go, go, go! Laney mouthed. Ignoring them, I added, "But no, I think my clowning days are over." Swallowing hard, I watched him remove two-thirds of the icing, then take a big bite of cupcake. *Without icing, he'll taste how bad it is for sure.*

"That's a shame. I was going to hire you for our next birthday party." He grinned, chewing.

Was he flirting?

Cole raised the mangled troll in cheers. "Good cupcakes."

"Really?" I couldn't hide my shock.

"You made them, right?"

I glared at my friends, who still watched intently. They must've told him. But wait...did that mean he'd inquired about me? Clearing my throat, I answered. "I did." Then an awkward chuckle escaped my lips. "You don't have to be nice, though. I know they're horrible."

"On the contrary." Cole popped the remnants of the cupcake into his mouth, then took another. With a slight tilt of his head, he captured my eyes. "I think they taste just right."

My cheeks warmed as a smile curled on my lips.

Adorable and real for the win.

SPICING THINGS UP

Dennis eyed the cylindrical tin in Sarah's hand. "What's that? Looks exotic."

"Hot chocolate. Got it at the World Flavour Market." Sarah scooped heaping spoonfuls of powder into three steaming mugs. "How many marshmallows do you want?"

"Mmm, I like mine extra lumpy. Thanks." Dennis inhaled the intoxicating aroma of cocoa. "Who's the third cup for?"

Sarah pulled out a glass bottle and poured some liquid courage into their beverages, then smiled wickedly. "You know how you've been wanting to spice things up? First with that roleplaying thing, then the furry costumes...then *you* wanted to get frisky in public – in a mall elevator."

Dennis's chin dropped to his chest. "Please don't bring that up again. I had no clue hitting the emergency stop button would trigger security cameras." He grimaced. "Or that they'd hold us until cops arrived to talk to us."

"Yes, well, at least everyone got a good show – much to my horror." Sarah stirred each cup, staring at the cocoa while she made lazy circles with the spoon. Then she shrugged dismissively. "But that's the thrill of it all, right? It definitely made me feel like a rebellious teenager."

Dennis perked up. "Yeah, exactly! Like we're teenagers all over again. Doing all the crazy things we never did the first time. Getting a little risky. A little wild." He leaned in closer, his eyebrows wiggling up and down.

His lips met hers in a kiss, but before he could get too carried away, she pulled back. "You know, I've been thinking about that other *wild fantasy* you keep mentioning..." Sarah's voice lowered to a sultry whisper. "I think I'm finally willing to give it a try."

Her husband's eyes grew as wide as the golf balls he lost after drinking too many beers on the back nine. An enthusiastic smile spread across his face. "Sweetie, this is going to be *amazing*."

"I think so, too." Sarah handed a steaming mug to Dennis, then turned to shout, "Jason, you can come out now!"

Dennis's mouth dropped open when a guest emerged from the pantry wearing a see-through crop top and ripped jeans. The mystery man's muscles bulged beneath the snug fibres.

"No time like the present. Let's spice things up." It was Sarah's turn to wiggle her eyebrows.

"Are you serious?" Dennis felt dizzy, quickly guzzling the contents of his mug – then immediately spitting it back out, fanning cool air into his scorched mouth. *"Hot,"* he mouthed.

Sarah took the beefy man's hand into her own. "Listen, I know I've been reluctant whenever you've brought it up before, but I'm willing to give it a try now. Maybe three isn't a crowd."

Dennis pulled Sarah aside. "Um, I kinda thought it would be another *woman* joining us."

Sarah nudged his ribs. "We have to start somewhere, right? We'll find a girl next time."

Dennis ran a hand over his face.

Jason winked, reaching out. "Looks like we're the bread in this sexy sandwich, eh Dennis?"

"Uh...yeah. I guess." Dennis flinched as Jason's fingers ran down his forearm.

Sarah giggled, slipping between the two men. "Mmm, yes! I want to get sandwiched. Hard."

Dennis backed into the kitchen island.

"I can't wait," Sarah purred, stretching up for a kiss.

"Uh..." He imagined his wife getting fondled by this hulk of a man. What if she liked his touch better?

"C'mon, Dennis. I promise I'll make it worth your while." Jason's eyes smouldered.

An all-new mental image assaulted Dennis's brain, causing him to recoil. He jumped back but had nowhere to go. His head clattered against the rack over the island, sending pots and pans flying. "Ow! Shit!"

"Are you okay?" Jason asked, concerned. The man's not-so-tiny hand caressed Dennis's back.

An involuntary groan escaped as Dennis slipped away with an awkward body roll. "I'm not sure I'm up for any sandwiches tonight."

"But this was your idea..." Sarah contemplated a moment, then offered, "Would you rather be the meat instead? I can be the bread." She turned to Jason, eyeing him up and down.

"No, no, no. No meat. No bread. No sandwich." Dennis side-stepped his way into the porch, peeking in from the doorway. "Actually, thinking more about it, this isn't such a good idea at all. Just you and me, Sarah—that's how it should be."

Sarah's hand dropped from caressing Jason's chest, shocked. "Are you sure?"

"Yep. Sure." He waved farewell with a stiff hand. "Drive home safe, Jason."

SARAH WALKED JASON TO THE FRONT DOOR, SMILING triumphantly. Once they both stood outside with the door shut behind them, Sarah handed the helpful escort some cash.

Jason crooked his fingers with a twisted grin. "And the bet?"

"You win. He totally chickened out." She shelled out more bills, slapping them into his hand.

"Most do." He chuckled, pocketing his payment.

"Bring in another woman? *Pish!*" Sarah shook her head. "This should straighten him out for a while."

One of Jason's eyebrows arched. "And if he asks again?"

"I've got your number." Sarah nodded firmly. "If Dennis gets to have another chick, I get to have another dick."

PINCHING PENNIES

Waiting in the wings, and brimming with anticipation, I proudly embodied the business end of a most dignified equine. Bluntly put, I was the horse's ass. I'd walked onto this grand stage for the past three nights in a row to perform as such. Moving my legs, stomping and swaying my body, each move completed just so. Through it all, I'd become a master of imitating a horse's natural movement. I even had a special chord I could pull to manipulate the tail, my favorite part, but it was imperative not to over-swish. The performance must always remain believable. It took months of focused practice and coordination with my 'better half' to pull this off. And when I say better half, I'm not talking about a wife.

A method actor to the core, I use every second of time to its fullest while awaiting my moment to shine. To better channel my character's personality, I would stomp, neigh, and whinny. Between scenes, I'd snack on Trigger's favorites — apples and carrots. I have even taken to chewing on long strands of hay. I personally didn't understand the appeal of hay, but it's not about me. It's about the character. To onlookers, it would appear that I talk to myself, but that's not quite right. Repeating my mantra over and over has helped me to find and keep the true soul of my character. "The horse is me, and I am the horse," I'd say. Well, the ass anyway.

Our production was completely new and unknown, written by one of our very own troupe members. It was a risk to put on a brand-new play, but we decided to go for it. Much to our surprise and delight, our little community theatre had been packed each night so far. The support from this town, never ceased to amaze.

"Are you ready, Andy?" My partner, Ted, asked in a hushed whisper.

"Of course. Are you?" I replied.

"Good to go."

For good measure, I chanted my mantra a few more times before adding, "Just remember, Ted. The horse is you, and you are the horse."

"Yeah, listen, you can quit with that crap now. I've heard it like a thousand times, and it wasn't even funny the first time. It's getting old."

"Oh, lighten up. I am just channeling my inner horse. The role of Trigger is very important." I wish he would take this more seriously. I also wished he might grow a soul, but no luck so far. Ted wasn't a very likeable sort. Every single year I secretly wished that he wouldn't get cast again, but this little troupe always needed bodies, and he always showed up.

"We play a damn horse. We stand on the stage." Through the shifting fabric, I could feel him shrug. "The biggest thing we do is trample Anna right before intermission. It's not that intense."

"You mean, Mrs. Snicklebatch," I corrected. "Anna's character is Mrs. Snicklebatch."

"Yeah, right. Whatever." I could sense the rolling eyes within his tone, even if I couldn't see them. I couldn't see much of anything, really. Within the dimly lit inner walls of the brown horse costume draped around us, all I could see was Ted's butt. And that view wasn't particularly inspiring for me.

Spending so much time with this guy had grown quite tiresome. We just simply didn't understand each other and likely never would. Ted had always been one of those guys-guys that thought his shit didn't stink. And I guess in his eyes, mine stank.

I felt a little rumble in my guts.

"Nobody knows horses like Duke. If there's anybody who can reach Trigger, he can," the housekeeper character said, played by a sweet middle-aged lady named Louise. She actually cleaned houses for a living and was thus perfectly cast. That was our cue. The lights cut out, and the curtain fell, the stage going to black. Multiple stage-hands scurried about, feet shuffling as they shifted the heavy coral set into place.

"Go time," Ted instructed. I followed his lead in a practiced step, our rhythms both measured and synchronized. A helpful stagehand used a flashlight to light our path. Looking through our tiny mesh viewing holes, we managed to maneuver ourselves within the coral.

This was the last scene before intermission, and it was a doozy. A crucial plot point. In the story, Duke, an old horse whisperer, tries to make a connection with us—er, the horse, but Mrs. Snicklebatch obnoxiously interrupts and upsets the process. She's a very unsavory character, in direct contrast to the lovely Anna who played her. Anna's long auburn hair, green eyes, and trim figure made my stomach flutter. She was kind, smart, and a bit of a jokester in rehearsals. I'd always had a secret crush on her but never worked up the courage to ask her out. She didn't even know I was alive, but I still felt it in my core that she could be perfect for me. If only Anna had been cast as ol' Triggers head. Now *she's* a better half I could stand to get behind.

Another grumble rolled through my abdomen. *That chili I had for supper must not be sitting right.*

The curtain raised, and the lights came back on. The scene took off, running like a finely-tuned machine. I tried not to get distracted by watching Anna mouthing the lines as she waited in the wings.

As practiced, Ted and I reacted to Duke's attentions, flinging the horse's head and prancing in a sidestep. Duke, a brooding cowboy-type, was played by Randy, an affable gentleman in his 40's. I think he was going for a Robert Redford vibe, but sadly it came off more like Chuck Norris in *Walker Texas Ranger*.

A sudden pain hit, like a big gas bubble was stuck in my large intestine. I bit back a groan as it shifted, anxiously waiting for it to subside. Thankfully, it did after a few moments.

The scene carried on, with Duke working his magic on Trigger. We ran in some circles, paced, and reared up a few times before finally settling down to his calming and (supposedly) awe-inspiring methods. Mrs. Snicklebatch came out then and called Duke away from us. For the rest of the scene, we just had to stay relatively still. Ted would bow the head occasionally, make the horse graze a bit, or give a few head shakes. I really didn't need to do much except stomp and occasionally swish the tail. Just a regular ol' horses' arse, hanging ten. So simplistic, yet, I manage to play it off perfectly.

In the meantime, my own arse was really starting to struggle. Whatever was eating away at my guts was sure doing a nasty job of it. Every few seconds or so, I was getting these cramping pains, some sharper than others. A particularly strong one struck, and my knees buckled slightly. The costume jostled around me.

"Keep still," Ted ordered in a hushed whisper.

A loud gurgle resonated from my belly, a heavy sensation moving through my lower half. *Seriously, what was in that chili?* Another gurgle had me instinctively squeezing my legs together, my butt cheeks so tight I could pinch pennies. This wasn't good.

Sweat was beginning to collect on my brow as I desperately fought to stay still and manage the horrible discomfort. The task was no small feat.

More gurgles broadcasted, accompanied by a sharp stab of pain. My knees buckled again, and Trigger's derriere dipped low while I grimaced within.

"What's wrong with you?" came Ted's irritated query.

I could feel an intense pressure building, my eyes widening with terror. I couldn't even answer. My entire being was wrapped up in a single-minded focus to contain what threatened to be unleashed.

BrraaAAAAAAPP...

I lost the battle. The loudest, most resounding fart I have ever experienced in my life came ripping out from between my buttocks. I froze, cringing with embarrassment.

Anna and Randy paused in their exchange, thrown off stride. Their voices stuttered, and through my little peephole, I could see that the front few rows were beginning to whisper. Raised brows, covered mouths, and several twittering snickers followed as everyone tried to guess which actor had passed wind. *Oh God, is that my aunt in the second row?*

I spied Anna glancing in my direction, clearly struggling to maintain her character's strict expression. What I couldn't tell, though, was if she was trying not to laugh or trying not to gag. My cheeks felt hotter with each passing second.

"What the hell, man?"

"I can't help it. I'm sorry," I groaned. The pungent smell wafted all around us, swirling and permeating every nook and cranny of the confined space. There was no hope to escape it.

"Damn, that's rancid," Ted grumbled, waving his free hand behind his back like a fan. He was desperately trying to push the tainted air back at me, nearly smacking my face in the process.

I tried to calculate how much time was left in the scene before we broke for intermission. Maybe five minutes, maximum? Our cue was coming up soon to bust loose from the corral and trample Mrs. Snicklebatch. It was the most important part of my role. Integral. I had to finish this scene.

Five minutes. I can do this.

Anna and Duke strolled over toward the corral. Of all the times in the world, this was the absolute worst for Anna to come closer to me. I normally maneuvered myself to be nearer to her on a regular basis, hoping she would finally realize I existed. But now was *not* one of those times.

Mrs. Snicklebatch was busy giving Duke the what-for, being a real grade-A bitch. Her southern accent was spot on as she overbearingly ordered Duke to get rid of the troublesome horse. And all the while, I was slowly dying inside.

The horse's ass was dancing now. I couldn't help it. Murmurs grew louder in the audience.

"Cool it, Andy!" Ted quietly snarled.

Only about three more minutes until we bust loose from the fence, but I was beginning to doubt I could make it. I pranced around to manage the pain as the gas bubbles tore my intestines.

There were giggles from the crowd. I had to get back on track, rectify this mess somehow.

Three minutes. I can make it.

"You see, Duke? This horse can't even stand still for goodness' sake. What a waste of good hay," Mrs. Snicklebatch commented pointedly, going off-script. She was trying to cover for me, bless her soul.

The bubbles became insistent, seeking their grand exit by the only available means. Pinching pennies just wasn't good enough. *Oh shit, oh shit, oh shit.*

PFFFttthwaaeeept...

The flatulence was painfully loud, high-pitched, and it felt wet. My jaw clenched. Ted simply growled in reaction, the horse's head shaking.

I heard more laughter rising from the audience, and through my peephole, I saw Randy shooting me a glare. Even Anna turned away for a moment, unable to hide her disgust. My ears felt like they were burning, probably red as tomatoes. I swallowed another groan, agonizing how this pain just wasn't relenting. Waves of cramps kept coming, one after the other, each one more insistent than the last. I needed relief fast, and I definitely wouldn't find it out here on this stage.

A stark realization slammed into my consciousness. I couldn't make it through the scene. If I didn't get to a bathroom soon, I was surely going to shit myself. Honest to God, shit myself.

The players dutifully kept going. Mrs. Snicklebatch continued gearing up to incite the required attack from Trigger, but her lines didn't sound as polished as normal. Her words were halting and awkward in their delivery. Both Randy and Anna were thoroughly distracted by the situation, their eyes warily keeping track of ol' Triggers gyrating back end.

I was faced with a grim decision, and I had maybe a minute left to decide. Either run off the stage or soil my underwear. The classic 'should I stay, or should I go' scenario. However, nothing about this felt classic. I could feel it coming. There was no question; it wouldn't be long. They always say in theatre that no matter what, the show must go on. But I mean, that's got to be within reason, right? There had to be an exception somewhere for explosive diarrhea.

My mind was frantic, weighing choice with consequence.

A few lines from now, I would have to run full speed to knock Anna over, and the thought of that was simply horrifying. Any amount of unclenching that occurred right now would surely result in utter calamity. But yet, I still hesitated. The last thing I wanted to do was wreck the show. My entire reputation as a thespian was at stake.

The pressure increased again, and I was shaking with the effort to contain the eruption.

Pffffeeeeee... A squeak of *mostly* air escaped.

That was it. Decision made.

"I'm sorry," I muttered to Ted as I forcefully shuffled backward, turning in my costume as I went. Only a handful of steps, and I would be off stage. Ted clumsily stumbled over his feet as he was dragged toward the wings.

"Andy!" he growled, trying to push back and keep me on stage. A short tug-o-war ensued, but I won as I lurched forward. Ted was thrown off balance and nearly crumpled but managed to shuffle along.

Shocked gasps and laughter rang out from the crowd as Randy and Anna fell silent.

We were finally off stage, and I scrambled to free myself of the equine shroud. I struggled with the little ties at the base of the costume. Another moist fart ripped out, and I felt like I could cry. I would never get another role ever again after this.

"Oh, no! Trigger has...escaped the paddock!" I heard Duke exclaim.

"Oh dear!" Mrs. Snicklebatch cried out overdramatically. I heard a thud, followed by frantic scuttering sounds. A bead of sweat rolled down the center of my back.

"Goodness me...Mrs. Snicklebatch has just fainted!" Duke projected awkwardly. "All of the...excitement...was just too much for her! There, there, Mrs. Snicklebatch. There, there."

The audience was sure getting a kick out of this. Hundreds of eyewitnesses. The news was going to spread like wildfire.

My last tie was finally free, and I flung the costume off my trembling body, making a beeline to the green room down the hall. Desperate fingers tugged at the top button of my slacks en route, but it wasn't coming loose. I bent at the waist to see better, focused on undoing the damn thing. My shoulder bounced off the wall, and I lost my footing, nearly going ass-over-teakettle, a little hot steam escaping in the process. Scrambling to right myself again, I darted the last few steps to the men's room. I locked myself inside and crashed down onto the toilet, letting loose a raw, guttural noise, the likes of which I had never uttered before.

Someone knocked on the door to ask if I was okay. I replied with a quick, "I'm fine."

Not long after, I heard the full cast come piling into the green room for intermission. I groaned, wiping the moisture from my forehead, and washed my hands. I double flushed the bowl's toxic contents and sprayed the room with an air freshener so fortuitously located on a shelf. The airy floral fragrance did little to save my nostrils from the noxious vapours fighting for dominance within the little room. Rolling my head atop my shoulders in an attempt to relieve the strain, I sighed. Sadly, I knew my bowels weren't finished yet; I could feel there would be more. I would have to go home.

I tried to decide what I would say to everyone. What could I say? I had zero explanation for what just happened. Every option I ran through my mind sounded ridiculous. So instead, I simply stayed locked in the bathroom, afraid to come out.

"Is Andy, okay? What was wrong with him?" I heard overheard Randy ask, sounding concerned.

"Where is he?" Anna questioned.

"In there," Ted said. "Probably crying." I imagined him pointing at the bathroom, a scowl on his face. That guy was never going to let me live this down.

A beat of silence followed, accompanied only by the creaking of the fridge door across the room.

"Hey, where's my water bottle?" Louise asked the group, but nobody owned up to taking it.

"What water bottle?" Anna asked.

"The one I had in the fridge, labelled with my initials." Louise closed the fridge door. "I hope nobody drank…" She stopped short.

My curiosity was piqued. I remember grabbing a water bottle when I first arrived.

"What about it, Louise?" Anna prodded.

"The bottle was premixed…for after our last show." Her voice sounded worried. A brief pause ensued before Louise took off again. "My husband told me to do it. He said it would be the most efficient way. You see, I have a very strict schedule to follow, and in order to get all the required solution into my system, I have to start drinking it right after the show ends tomorrow. The doctor said it's a brand-new product, the first of its kind to have *zero* flavor. Revolutionary stuff. It is supposed to be wonderful, so I am looking forward to that. Not that I'm looking forward to a colonoscopy! I meant the taste. Usually, this stuff tastes horrible. Just horrible. I had to do this a few years ago, and it was so hard to—"

"Louise, I'm sorry to stop you, but—"

"Get to the point already," Ted barked, cutting Anna off. As much as I hated Ted, I kind of agreed with him this one time. Louise, as charming as she was, tended to ramble.

"Oh…so sorry. My clean-out solution was in that water bottle!"

Clean-out solution? My eyes widened before clamping shut.

Another beat of silence followed.

"Well, that might explain a few things," Ted quipped flatly. A lot of muffled muttering followed after, impossible to make out.

Louise's pleasant voice penetrated the closed-door moments later. "Andy, darling?" Are you okay in there?"

"Yes," I answered, hanging my head low.

"Listen, did you happen to drink a bottle of water from the fridge today? Did you notice if it had initials written on the label?"

"The bottle I drank is in the recycling bin."

There were rustling sounds, followed by an "Aha! There it is." *Shit.*

My heart fell into my feet. How could I have been so stupid?

"He really is a horse's ass after all," Ted joked with a laugh. My shoulders sagged.

"Ted, that's enough," Anna snipped at him. "It was an accident."

"What? Clearly, the guy can't even read. And then he screws up the whole show!"

"You're such a dick, Ted."

"Oh my. I should've marked it better," Louise said. "I feel horrible."

I quietly opened the door and walked out of the room. There was no graceful way to handle this situation. I just needed to leave.

I saw Louise holding her empty bottle with a pitying look of sympathy in her eyes. Randy smiled kindly while Ted shot me a belittling thumbs up. I cringed inside.

I couldn't bear to look at Anna.

"I need to go home." One of the stagehands could easily take my place for the last half of the show. Anybody could, really. There's no use kidding myself about it anymore. I was just the lesser half of a stupid horse. Demoralized, I averted my gaze, grabbed my bag, and slipped out.

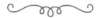

THE NEXT DAY, I ARRIVED BACK AT THE THEATRE WITH A freshly bruised ego and a sore behind. Nobody was around, all likely in makeup. I was thankful to be alone; I planned to avoid interacting with everybody as much as humanly possible. I just needed to get through this last show, and then I would never have to see any of them again. Maybe I could drive into the city and join a theatre troupe there instead?

I opened the fridge to take out a water bottle, very methodically inspecting it before putting it to my lips. It was then that I noticed a package sitting on the green room table, with a sticky note on top. Curious, I read the handwritten message, quickly realizing it was for me.

ANDY: THESE ARE FOR YOU. THE HORSES ASS IS YOU, AND YOU ARE THE HORSES ASS. TED

I ripped at the tacky Christmas wrapping haphazardly taped together around the parcel. A dejected sigh escaped my throat when I saw the contents. A package of Depends. "That's funny, Ted. Just hilarious..."

Did they all share Ted's sentiments? My thoughts swirled, suddenly considering how silly I must've appeared to everybody, taking my tiny role so seriously. Was I just a big laughing stock?

I once believed that my penchant for method acting was completely fine. Tonnes of big-name actors did it all the time, so why couldn't I? It was fun. But I now realized the error of my logic. Like a smack in the face. I was no big-name actor—and all it did was brand me as a weirdo.

Perhaps I'll just find another theatre troupe after all. I'll join somewhere that I can start fresh.

I hung out in the wings until it was my time to suit up again, speaking to nobody. Louise came by and gave my arm a gentle squeeze, very motherly. Anna passed me a few times, too, smiling compassionately, which bothered me even more. Pity was not the kind of attention I wanted from that beautiful creature.

Ted made a few more snide comments, thinking he was such a comedian. Not a surprise. I chose to ignore him. I didn't want to give him the satisfaction of seeing that it was bothering me. It wasn't an easy task since we had to operate Trigger together, but I did the best I could.

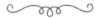

THE SHOW RAN RELATIVELY SMOOTHLY UNTIL THE LAST couple scenes of the second half. In the storyline, our character, Trigger, ends up being rehabilitated and winning a big race. In the current scene, we're just supposed to stand on stage holding still, except for our usual intermittent horse-like mannerisms, of course. A large flowery wreath gets draped over our withers while Duke and Mrs. Snicklebatch, who was now a changed woman, both stood proudly beside their prize winner.

I heard a loud gurgle echo within the fabric walls surrounding us. Instinctively, I looked down at my stomach with immediate concern. The gurgle occurred again, but I felt nothing. It definitely wasn't me.

Ted shifted oddly up ahead, his hips moving around uncomfortably. *What the hell?*

The front half of the horse soon began prancing. I became worried since I was perched directly behind him. Not that I wanted to see it, but in my current situation, I couldn't help but notice his butt was really clenching.

"Fuck man, my guts... Did you do this?" His whisper was harsh, enraged.

"What? No."

Brrruuubbph...

My entire expression scrunched. "Aw, c'mon." My poor face had a front-row show, and my goodness, those vapors were rank. At least when I split my cheeks yesterday, it wasn't into his bloody face.

As the farts and discomfort intensified, I experienced a very distinct sense of déjà-vu.

It didn't take long before Ted was unceremoniously dragging me off the stage, accompanied by a whole new slew of spectator giggles. This time, it was me who scrambled to get back out there, partnered by the same stagehand from last night.

I wondered what the crowd must be thinking. Two shows in a row. I absolutely dreaded reading the shit reviews we were going to get.

AFTER THE PLAY ENDED, ALL THE ACTORS GATHERED IN THE greenroom. Well, except Ted. Many different discussions flew around the room. I sat quietly in the corner chair, listening to everybody mull over what had happened. Nobody had any clue this time.

Louise swore up and down that she'd kept her clean-out solution in her bag. The only thing anybody recalled seeing Ted consume was his usual protein shake at intermission.

A few people looked in my direction, and all I could do was shrug. I'm sure they wondered if I was behind it.

There was nothing left to say. I picked up my bag and headed out, muttering my farewell. I was feeling somewhat relieved that this whole production had come to a close. But as I plodded down the stairs toward the door, I heard my name called from behind. Turning, I saw Anna rushing to catch up to me, her coat on and purse slung over her shoulder.

"Andy! I just wanted to say that you shouldn't feel bad about what happened. Nobody blames you."

"Thanks. You're too kind," I gave a weak smile in return, surprised she was speaking to me.

"It was a horrible mix-up yesterday, and it could have been any one of us just as easily as you."

"Maybe."

"And don't let Ted's note bother you. Nobody else here cares that you're into method acting. Eating hay is a little odd, yes...but we're all a little odd. We're actors." She waved it off casually.

"Well, I think my hay-chewing days are over."

"Whatever works for you." She nodded in understanding, pulling on a toque. "But regardless, Ted shouldn't have said those things. Or left that package for you." She huffed. "He's such an asshole." Anna held out her hand to me. "I'm officially apologizing for him."

"Thanks again," I replied as I took her hand and shook it. "But I'm sure he *won't* appreciate that gesture." I couldn't help but chuckle.

"Yes, well..." A mischievous look sparkled in her eyes as a sly grin flashed. "I don't think he will appreciate *any* of my gestures." She fished for something in her purse, soon revealing a glimpse of a white plastic container. "A clean-out solution mixes perfectly with a protein shake, wouldn't you say?"

She winked. My mouth fell agape, connecting the dots. "Anna, you didn't—"

"Shh. It'll be our little secret. It's good for that man to get knocked down a peg or two. He was a particularly horrible brand of douche after you left last night. Randy, Louise, and I were sick of it."

"Randy and Louise too?" I paused for a moment, the corners of my mouth tugging upward. "You know, I still suffered tonight. Through sheer proximity. My face...Ted's butt..."

"Yeah, we didn't think that one through." She tucked a stray hair behind her ear. "Sorry."

"It's okay." I shrugged. "Too bad there isn't any hazard pay, though."

She laughed at my joke, burying the bottle of powder back into her purse. Still stunned, I didn't quite know what else to say. I couldn't believe they all did something like that for my benefit. I felt...touched.

"Anyway, maybe now he won't come back for next season's show." Anna crossed her fingers and walked over to the exit. "Will I see you at the cast party tomorrow? I hope you will come."

I nodded, and she flashed me one last smile before whisking out the door.

In that moment, I felt my spirit's lift. Don't get me wrong, my mind still reeled over the recent events, but it didn't seem as overwhelming. Not everyone felt like Ted did after all. And, the fact that Anna just took the time to try and make me feel better...that meant a lot.

A lightbulb suddenly switched on in my head, and an unfamiliar surge of confidence drove me to whip the door open. I called after her. Why not, right? Nothing else could be as humiliating as what happened to me out on that stage. Anna stopped, turning around. The words came flying out of my mouth before I had any chance to talk myself out of it. "Would you like to get a cup of coffee with me sometime?"

An adorable smile spread into her eyes. "Sure, that sounds fun."

"Okay, great! Well, I'll see you tomorrow." I waved as I watched Anna get into her vehicle and depart. Did that just happen?

What a crazy couple of days.

Heading to my truck, I swung open the door and slid into the driver's seat. A slow smile spread across my face as I conducted a mental recap. Ted had received his just desserts, my bowels were *very* thoroughly cleansed, and it turned out I didn't need to find another theatre troupe after all. *Plus*, Anna was finally aware of my existence...

I guess nearly shitting oneself had some advantages after all.

TO FLUFF, OR NOT TO FLUFF

Take the Christmas tree out of its box—check. Ensure the base is connected and secure—check. The part I hated the most came next: fluffing the branches. *Ugh, so tedious.* But it was worth the effort to have a more realistic looking tree. It was Steve's and my first Christmas together as a married couple, and I wanted everything to look perfect.

"Need some help?" my husband asked cheerfully.

Steve set down the beer he'd just cracked. I shot him a look, sliding a coaster beneath the bottle before a moist ring marked my coffee table.

"Oh yeah, coasters. I'm sure that will become a habit eventually," he said with a grin.

We were still working out the kinks in our daily marital routine. I'd been learning that when two thirty-year-old individuals joined together, each with well-ingrained habits, it made finding a new normal an interesting task.

"Yeah, sure. Start on that side, and we'll meet in the middle." I smiled, thankful.

Setting to work, I furiously pulled at countless faux-spruce sprigs, arranging their spread in all different directions. The fewer gaps, the better.

At last, twenty minutes later, I reached the halfway point. I was about to celebrate a job well done, when, instead of running into layered rows of spunky twigs, I encountered exactly the opposite. The branches were abnormally flat. And not just a shoved-in-a-box kind of flat but rather an I've-been-very-meticulously-flattened flat. *What the...*

Peering around the tree, my eyes targeted the enemy like lasers. There was Steve, diligently working away on limbs I'd already finished—flattening freshly fluffed bows into pancakes. *No!*

"Stop!" I rounded the tree to confront him. "Don't you dare touch another branch!"

Steve froze, eyes filled with confusion. His hands slowly lifted in surrender.

"Notice a difference here?" I pointed to his side of the tree, and then to my remaining examples of puffed perfection.

He looked, then shrugged. "What?"

"You're supposed to fluff them! Like these, see? Who has flat branches on a Christmas tree?"

"Oh...oops." He rubbed his neck, realizing he'd been undoing all my progress. "Well, I grew up with them flat. Honestly, that's what I thought you were doing."

"*Really?* NO!" My hands planted on my hips. "Fake trees need to be fluffed, period. Otherwise, it just looks like a bunch of spindly twigs stuck on a pole."

"Okay, okay." Steve gave me a crisp salute, smirking. "I can see you're much more passionate about this than I, so it is my official decree that our tree shall *never* be flat."

"Good. Thank you."

We stared at each other, lips slowly curling as the ridiculousness of the situation sank into our consciousnesses. Then, as if on cue, we both dissolved into chuckles.

Newlywed problems.

Shaking my head, I stretched up to kiss his cheek. "Well..." I looked at the tree, then back to him. Channeling my inner Vanna White, I highlighted his handy work with the wave of a hand. "*I'm* not redoing all of *that.*"

Steve's eyes widened. "But—"

I grabbed his beer, took a swig, then plopped onto the couch. "You, *oh great flattener*, best get fluffing."

MR. REGRET

I was drunk. Not the good kind either. Whisky did this to me every time, turned me into a blubbering black hole of self-pity and depression. Nothing short of a miracle could break me out of this funk.

The night started out like it always did. I slathered makeup on my face, styled my hair just right, and squeezed my few-too-many pounds into a revealing little number. All to attract a still-single-but-not-a-loser member of the opposite sex. A rare species in my current age bracket.

I went to the usual club with a couple of girlfriends from work. They were single and hunting, just like I was. We danced flamboyantly and more than a little too sexy, hoping Mr. Right would be drawn in by sheer animal magnetism. I scoped the room, unenthused by the candidates, but perhaps tonight would be that one night I'd discover a diamond in the rough. I always told myself that.

There were no diamonds.

Instead, I met Nick and Jimmy, who undoubtedly still lived in their parents' basements, praying to finally lose their virginity to a real woman.

"Did you know that video gaming can cause carpal tunnel?" Jimmy had asked.

I doubted it was the video games that did that.

Christian cha-cha'd into our circle next, with awkward finger pointing and a tan line where his ring normally resided, for goodness' sake. A real slick-haired smooth-talker looking for an easy lay. I mean, I'm desperate, but not that desperate.

By midnight we'd had enough. I decided to walk home, waving goodnight to my friends as they got into a taxi. My apartment was a fair distance away, fifteen minutes on foot, but I figured the cool autumn air might do me good. Or it wouldn't, and I'd simply catch pneumonia and die. That worked too. *Boy, the whisky is really working its magic tonight.*

I popped into a 24-hour convenience store to buy a chocolate bar. My drug of choice. Wandering down the aisle, the latest edition of Architect Magazine stood out to me. I winced. There he was—his damn face right on the cover. Looking as sexy as ever with his perfectly groomed goatee and salt n' pepper hair. Jason Whitfield. Father Time had been kind to him.

I remember how perfect things had been twenty years ago... I was young and perky, just finishing up a hard-earned University degree, bright-eyed and raring to go. Not to mention being thirty-five pounds lighter. Jason was my boyfriend, the man of my dreams, my Mr. Right. We were meant for each other, but then I had to go and mess it all up. Something made me break up with him, but I couldn't for the life of me imagine what that might've been. I was so stupid back then. Too naive to realize what I'd lost until it was too late.

I snatched the magazine off the rack and thrust a few bills at the cashier, already biting into a Mars bar. Voracious for creature comfort, there was another stuffed in my pocket for later.

I stumbled my way down the sidewalk, a few too many drinks sloshing around inside me. Staring at the magazine riled up the bitterness. I heard Jason was still single, hailed as one of the most eligible bachelors in the country. Last year I sent him an email, thinking we could rekindle the romance. Maybe he missed me too?

I never received a response.

What did it even matter at this point? Really. I had a cat who hated me, a job I dreaded going to, and the only romance I ever experienced was on the television screen. Unless I counted the frequent and rhythmic banging emanating from next door. From the muffled accompanying moans and whimpers, it was clear my neighbour had no lack of romance in *his* life. I tried not to feel jealous when I listened in, popcorn in hand. What was wrong with me?

The only thing that brought me joy in this shit life was my mom, and she passed away six months ago. She was the only one who gave a crap about me. Honestly, I don't know why I didn't just end it all then. It's been so hard without her.

Thinking back, I can pinpoint the day that everything started to go downhill. It was June 16th, 1997. The day I walked away from a millionaire.

And it just kept rolling from there.

Nearing the river, I wiped at the tears and melting mascara as a fresh sob racked my shoulders. Jason was the one that got away. The one I *let* get away.

Twenty-two years had passed, spent dreaming of what might have been. Too many long years of regret, every moment of it leading me here. Bawling my eyes out, I sat on the ledge of a single-lane bridge only a few short minutes from my house.

It wasn't as impressive or scenic a locale as I'd imagined for my grand exit, nor was the bridge a beautiful feat of engineering mastery, but it was plenty high to be effective. Tonight, that was enough for me.

Railroad tracks leading to unknown places stretched out below, soon to be decorated with a warm shade of red.

"I am over this!" I cried out into the stillness. "I'm done." I set my jaw firm in my decision. It was time to end the madness.

I pulled off my high heels, setting them aside on the sidewalk. No need to damage a perfectly good pair of *Jimmy Choo's*. Standing up, I leaned back against the rail, clutching it as an abnormally strong gust of wind tested my balance. Seconds later, another wave of air crashed over me, blowing my hair and clothes like a flag in the prairies. Was a storm moving in? It had been calm all night until now. Looking up, nothing but stars twinkled above.

Not a hint of a cloud. *Odd.*

"Enough distractions Linda," I ordered myself with a head shake. It was time to get back to the task at hand. "Let's just get this over with. The world will be thankful," I muttered. A fresh batch of tears streamed down my cheeks as I stared at the ground, preparing for the fall. My mind spun, thinking about all the things I didn't get to do, all the ways I wasted my existence, and how nothing I could do would ever make it right again. My grip slowly loosened, the cold metal railing sliding beneath my fingertips.

"Are you sure you want to do that?"

Startled by the deep voice behind me, my hands flexed in shock. As I reclaimed my hold, I glanced over my shoulder to see who was there. Heart pounding, I felt vulnerable, exposed. Fear took control as I saw a strange man standing there. A tall, sharply dressed man only feet away. His hands were tucked into his pockets as he calmly smiled.

He could have a knife in his pocket.

"Stay back! Get away from me." I turned my body against the rails to face the intruder, eyes trained on him. The man put his hands up, both empty.

"I mean you no harm, Linda."

"How do you know my name?" Hooking an elbow around one of the metal rails, I frantically dug through my purse. My fingertips finally touched a cylindrical container of pepper spray. Like American Express, I never leave home without it. "Just back off!" I wanted to die in my own way, on my own terms. Not at the hands of some pervy, stalker serial killer.

As I whipped out the cannister, my foot simultaneously slipped off the edge, jarring my body downward. A splice of a scream escaped my lips before I felt two firm hands grab my shoulders. Pervy stalker man's gaze locked with mine, his eyes focused and unwavering. The steady support allowed my foot to regain purchase on the cold concrete.

"I'm not going to hurt you," he soothed. "Come now." He nodded toward the safe side where he stood. Taking my hand, I was guided back over the rails.

Once my feet were back on the sidewalk, my heart rate slowing, I couldn't help but notice his striking features. The bluest eyes I had ever seen, a crisp, pointed nose, and a meticulously trimmed beard that faded into his sideburns. He had two streaks of colour in his dark wavy hair, one white and one red, each running parallel to the other, running back from his hairline. A curious style choice.

"Who are you?" I asked shakily, suddenly feeling the nighttime chill on my skin. Or maybe I was in shock.

"I am a friend. My name is irrelevant."

His smile was alarmingly charming. Some of my fear ebbed.

"Oh, no, it is *very* relevant. Who are you?" I managed a weak smile looking into those ice-blue eyes, and unable to help myself, I added, "And are you single?"

The man chuckled, shaking his head. "I don't have any interest in women."

Ohhh...got it. That made sense, with the nice clothes and meticulous grooming. "Sorry, I hope I didn't offend you. I actually know a couple of guys from the gym that would love to meet you, I'm sure."

"Uh, no, I have no interest in men either. I don't date, but thank you for asking." He let me go, watching to be certain I was stable. I didn't feel particularly steady, my body still trembling from the experience, but my mind felt sharper now. The alcoholic depression was rapidly clearing from my thoughts. I glanced back over the side of the bridge, contemplating what nearly happened. Oddly, I felt a mixture of relief and sadness.

"What are you doing here? It's like 3:00am. Are you going to kill me?"

"Isn't that what you want? To die?"

The fear rose within me again, despite his temperate expression. My limbs stiffened, preparing to run as I stepped back. "That's my business." I raised the pepper spray still locked in my hand, preparing to squirt and run. "Nobody wants to be *murdered.*"

He raised his hands again, shaking his head. "I am not here to kill you. I heard your distress, and I've come to offer you a solution. An option."

My face twisted in confusion. "What?"

"If you had the chance to go back to do one thing over again, would you take it?"

What? My brain hurt.

"Listen, buddy, I think you need to head back to your padded room, okay?"

His eyes twinkled with amusement as he raised a hand, snapping his fingers. I squinted as a blinding light flashed, whitewashing all of our surroundings. The light faded just as quickly, but when my vision reacclimated, I was not where I should've been. Warm air enveloped me, easing the goosebumps on my exposed skin.

Where the hell am I?

"This is the hallway of decisions." The man announced, still standing in front of me. Slipping his hands back in his pockets, he grinned. "*Your* hallway, to be exact."

"Undo it." I looked around, panicking. This was too bizarre to be real. I stood in the middle of a long yellow hallway—so yellow it could squeeze lemon. The blazing citrus walls were lined with old wooden doors, the heavy kind you don't find in stores anymore. "Undo it now. Take me back. Do the snappy thing again." My heart was pounding a drum solo in my chest.

"Let me explain first. When I'm done, if you still want to return to the bridge, I will most definitely take you back." He spread his arms wide then, palms up. "Deal?"

I couldn't believe what was happening. Is this Heaven, or maybe Hell? Did I jump already and not remember? Or maybe this guy attacked and drugged me, and I was trapped in his twisted torture chamber. My eyes darted all around, trying to make sense of it all. The urge to run swelled, but I had no clue where I was.

My gaze flitted back to he-who-shall-not-be-named, who continued to regard me calmly. Hands back in his pockets, he leaned forward, meeting my gaze. I tried to look away but found I couldn't. It was like an emotional shift was forced upon me, an irresistible pull commanding my attention. Something soft glimmered in his eyes, hypnotic and inviting. My heartbeat slowed, and my nerves eased. This fantastical stranger was urging me to trust him, and I was listening.

"Relax," he cooed softly, gaze steady.

"Okay," I said on a breathy sigh.

After a moment of silence passed, his pacifying demeanour shifted dramatically.

"Great." He straightened, clapping his hands together cheerfully. The man's entire expression brightened as he genially guided me forward. He'd make an excellent hotel manager.

What a quirky guy.

"These are the doors of regret." He pointed down the hallway. "Everybody's doors are different. Some have too many to count, while others only have one or two."

"Doors of regret," I repeated skeptically, brows furrowed. I counted seven doors in total, spread out down the hall.

"That's right, and these are *your* doors." He walked over to the first, plopping a hand onto the brass handle. He waved me closer, "Come on."

Eyes constantly scanning, I followed. "Is this some kind of elaborate prank? Are there hidden cameras around here somewhere?" I examined my surroundings, eyes squinting. "And can we do something about the blinding yellow walls?"

"Oh, yes, of course." Raising his hand, he snapped his fingers once more. The paint rippled like a wave down the length of the hall, the colour fading into a pale shade of violet. "Is this better?"

Purple wasn't a particular favourite of mine, but it was definitely better than neon lemonade. "Yes, thank you."

"Very good." The consummate host, the man snapped his fingers yet again, opening the door this time. He peered inside briefly before motioning for me to do the same. "Does this look familiar to you?" I followed his gaze, eyes widening in a double-take.

It was the cafe I got a job waitressing in when I was 17. I practically grew up in that place, and it was right there in front of me, plain as day. "Incredible. Barny's burned down years ago." Wondering whether it was a screen or a hologram, I tried to wave a hand through the image, but the man quickly blocked me.

"No touching. Just watch," he encouraged.

I saw myself bussing a table, then heading toward a booth to take an order. I cringed as I heard a telltale laugh ring out like nails on a chalkboard. *Oh, I know when this is.*

Trudy, the owner of that horrible laugh, sat with all her popular flunkies. She was twittering on about how awesome her new car was (that her rich daddy bought), what jewellery she had purchased recently, and the expensive clothing she wore. Trudy hated me, and I didn't particularly care for her either since she constantly went out of her way to make my school experience as miserable as possible. I wasn't cool enough to breathe in her airspace.

"Oh, look, it's *Linda*. It makes sense *you* would be the one to serve me." She cackled, highlighting my low-class need to work. She proceeded to spell out her overly specific order, light on this and substitute this with that...and only glacier water in a bottle, with a straw. She was watching her figure before a big date with the quarterback, apparently. With a hair flip, she asked pointedly, "Can you manage that, Lin-*Duh*? And you better not screw it up. My dad can get you fired in a heartbeat."

I watched my younger self walk away seething. "Can I go in there?" I asked, stepping forward. Suddenly, I felt invigorated by what these doors might mean. A do-over. I knew what came next, so I wondered, how could I still mess with Trudy's head while simultaneously stopping my old self?

"Wait," he held an arm out, holding me back. The vision beyond the door fast-forwarded like an old recorded VHS movie. Young Linda retrieved the order sitting on the pass bar. She took Trudy's plate into the back and promptly spit in the food when nobody was looking. I looked away, embarrassed, cheeks turning red. My nameless guide raised an eyebrow.

"That wasn't my finest moment, I know." I shrugged. "I felt really bad after, too. That brief moment of satisfaction didn't last. Trudy was a bitch for sure, but stooping to that low was a huge stain on my otherwise ethical working life. The guilt has haunted me."

"And that is precisely why you are here. Now you understand more clearly what lies behind these doors. Each one contains one of your most impactful regrets. Things that you might want to do over if given the chance." He pulled the door closed.

"So, I can go back and change all of my regrets?"

"It doesn't quite work like that." He led me to the next door down the hall. This one had a silver doorknob. "There are some strings attached. I am offering you the option to relive *one* of your worst regrets. Only one. So, you must choose wisely."

"Why only one?"

"We will talk more. First, go ahead and check every door. However, do not walk through any of them yet." His face was very serious. "If you pass a threshold in any way, even if it's just a pinky finger, that becomes your choice. Once the decision is made, it cannot be undone."

"Okay..." I felt nervous turning the silver handle, but that feeling was quickly replaced with frustration when the door refused to budge. Uselessly, I tried again, then remembered all the finger-snapping this mysterious man was so very fond of.

"So, what, I just snap it open like you did?" I snapped my thumb and middle finger with gusto. Nothing happened. "Open sesame!" I commanded, giving it another try, to no avail.

The man shook his head, robust rumbles of laughter escaping his perfectly formed lips. "Leave the snapping to me, Linda. You will need to use the keys."

We stared at each other for a moment. Then another. His smile remained placid while mine twitched with growing confusion.

Finally, I broke the silence. "Um, so, are you going to give them to me?"

"You've had them all along." With his head, he nodded toward my purse.

"What?" My fingers began rummaging immediately. Sure enough, there was a metal ring with seven ornately designed keys on it. They were heavy like cast iron. How had I not noticed?

"Let me know when you've chosen," my guide added, then meandered off.

I turned back to the door, whispering, "Here we go." After

trying six of the keys, I finally found the right one. Turning the silver handle, the latch clicked, and the door swung open.

Only one...

I watched the scenes play out behind each successive door, cringing more and more as the experiences were revived before my eyes. The silver-handled door led to my junior high dance when I'd exited the bathroom with a small piece of dress tucked in my underwear.

A pewter doorknob opened into an important job interview ten years ago when I'd broken down crying. So embarrassing.

The modern chrome knob revealed that time I ignored and walked past a homeless man in the middle of winter, then recognized him on the news the next day. He'd died. Giving him my extra coins might not have changed anything, but I always wondered *what if?*

I turned a crystal-like door handle, and my cheeks flushed as I watched a seven-year-old me pumping fake coins into a gumball machine, nearly emptying the whole container before my backpack was full.

A golden knob highlighted the single time I forgot to put money into the lottery pool at work, and they freaking won 150,000 dollars. Every day thereafter, I'd cursed at the copy of the lottery ticket they proudly pinned up in the staffroom. I still kicked myself over that. *23 45 98 12 72.* To this day, I can see those lotto numbers in my head —burned into my subconscious. I've always had a good mind for numbers.

With each new door, I held my breath, waiting to see him. Jason. But he hadn't shown up yet. Now, standing before the very last door, I took a deep breath. This had to be it.

An ornately crafted wrought iron handle garnished the dark wooden door. I depressed the flat button lever on top and pulled. Dim light shone on my face as I recognized the inside of Jason's car parked outside his apartment building. *This is it.*

A much younger me sat in the passenger seat, feeling torn after going to dinner and a movie. Jason invited young Linda up to his place. She hemmed and hawed. He caressed her thigh and said he was falling in love, leaning over for a kiss, but young Linda stopped him.

"What are you doing, you stupid cow!" I yelled through the doorway, but it made zero impact on the scene playing out. I watched as if I were sitting in the backseat.

Young Linda explained she couldn't continue seeing him, saying he was a great guy but she simply couldn't stay in the city after graduation. I saw Jason's face fall, then quickly grow irritated. He was angry about how the last few months were a giant waste of time. She offered to try long distance, but he didn't go for it. Jason said he couldn't live like that, not seeing her all the time. He begged her to just come up for one drink so they could talk about it more.

He is perfect for you. You're blowing it!

The naive idiot version of me just sat there, with her poker-straight hair pulled into a ponytail and an awkward expression on her face. She was wearing a very unfortunate jean jacket and flowery-skirt combo, still dressing true to her farmgirl roots, contrary to popular styles of the time. Young Linda turned him down. He got angry and refused to drive her home, so she got out to walk.

"It's a wonder a guy like Jason was even interested in you at all," I muttered to myself. "He was so out of your league yet wanted you anyway...and then you decided to blow him off." I growled. The vision faded to black and then restarted from the beginning. "He was in love with us, for goodness' sake! You've never found another man as high calibre as him. And you never will."

I stopped myself. *Why am I standing here spouting off like this? I can change it.*

I waved to my silent observer down the hall.

In a single blink, he appeared at my side. I stumbled back a step, surprised. "S-so, Mr. Regret man," *for lack of a better name,* "I've chosen. How does this work? I walk through, redo it all, and then come back to see how my life turned out?" I imagined waking up next to Jason tomorrow morning. Maybe even having a couple kids running around the house.

"Mr. Regret...I like that." He smirked. "When you walk through the door, you'll be back as you once were, reliving the moment you've just seen here." He motioned to the door. "But once you do, you can never return to your old life. As I said before, it cannot be undone."

"But what if I can't fix it? I don't get to try again or just give up and resume my old life?"

"That is the conundrum. What happens beyond the door is out of my control. I am only able to give you the opportunity. Whether it's worth the risk is for you to decide. If you choose not to enter a doorway, I will take you back to the bridge."

"Does anybody ever say no?"

"The odd time."

"Why?"

"There are certain things they wouldn't dare change. Fear. Not worth the energy. There are many reasons." Mr. Regret shrugged.

I considered that information, letting it soak in. "Why did you pick me?"

"We screen for hopelessness," he replied matter-of-factly.

I wanted to be offended by that answer, but I *was* just about to throw myself off a bridge when we met. All things considered, hopeless seemed fairly appropriate.

"We?" I prodded.

"It's a big world, and I am but one being."

Huh, so there are more like him. "Are you an angel or something?"

He shot me a look belying tested patience—the first real emotion I'd seen from him yet. It didn't last long, though; his demeanour quickly flipped back to the calm and soothing. "You may call me that if you wish. But not everyone will."

"Why—"

"Do you know what you'd like to do, or would you like a moment to think it over?" He cut me off, anticipating more questions.

I looked down at my hands, running all the pros and cons through my mind. A man who loves me and the endless possibilities that would come with that versus the useless routine that I'm living now. What cons could there be? I had nothing to lose. Mr.

Regret should already know that. Otherwise, he wouldn't have found me.

"I am walking through this door."

"Excellent. Best of luck to you." His smile was broad, hands clasped behind his back.

I turned back to the door, pumping myself up inside. *I can't believe this is really happening.* Just as I moved my leg across the threshold, Mr. Regret piped up again.

"Oh, one other tiny little thing. There is always a side effect from the continuum shift. Usually very minor. Nothing to worry about." He breezed through that statement very quickly, then waved me onward, his charming smile unfazed.

With one leg in and one leg out, I had concerns. "Wait, what kind of side effe—" But my train of thought was lost mid-sentence as a powerful force grabbed onto my limb. It was like quicksand, sucking me deeper into the doorway. Panic filled every crevice of my body as I looked frantically to my nameless recruiter for assistance. My eyes felt so wide, my eyebrows probably touched my hairline.

"It's normal. Don't fight it. Just let it take you where you want to go."

It didn't feel safe. Like I was on the wrong end of an industrial-strength vacuum cleaner. My other leg was being pulled in now. "Are you telling me the truth?"

"Don't be afraid, Linda." He rested his hand on the doorknob, preparing to close it behind me. "Best wishes in your new life."

My hips were being sucked in. I leaned forward, my heart racing. Had I been duped? Could this be some kind of experimental device that is slowly sucking the life out of me? I had major second thoughts, but I doubted I had a choice in the matter anymore. My chance to bolt was too far gone. My waist was suctioned in, the rib cage next on the docket. I suddenly remembered my question and spat it out again. "What kind of side effects?"

"Oh, yes. Usually, it's just a minor change in your body, or on rare occasions, a foreign object somewhere inside you."

"*What?* You should really tell people this stuff up front, serious-ly!" I was appalled. "Like a *large* foreign object?"

My chest was being dragged in deeper, and my mind was frantic, my breathing shallow.

"No, very small. Always removable by doctors."

I screamed involuntarily as my shoulders were pulled in, the forceful energy now grasping at my arms too.

But I didn't feel any pain, which was promising. Maybe it would be okay after all. Mr. Regret was still standing there, watching and smiling at me so encouragingly. I mean, he saved me before, so he can't be evil. *Right?* My internal monologue helped to battle my rampant worst-case scenario thoughts. Slightly.

Mr. Regret leaned over to lock eyes with me, his mystical gaze working hard to soothe. Once more, I couldn't look away and instantly felt my body relax. It seemed to be his special power, and at this moment, I was thankful for the relief. That familiar shimmer appeared in his irises again, and then his face was gone. My head sank through the doorway, and everything disappeared from view.

I OPENED MY EYES; MY HEAD FELT A LITTLE FUZZY. LOOKING down, I saw my 23-year-old body sitting in the passenger seat, ankles crossed, the flowery skirt draped over my thighs. I lifted my hands to inspect them, wiggling my fingers, in awe that I was in control.

It really happened. I'm really here.

"Everything okay?" Jason looked at me funny, pulling the car to park in front of his apartment building. I met his gaze and nearly melted.

"Ah...um yes," I answered, lowering my hands. A smile found my lips easily. "Just checking out my nails, ya know."

"So, we're here. Tonight, was so much fun. I love spending time with you." His dimples showed when he grinned. "Would you like to come up for a drink? I'm not ready to say goodnight yet."

His laugh was like music to my ears, his warm hand on my thigh a symphony. He leaned in toward me, and I closed my eyes. I locked my fingers together in my lap to make sure no previous-life inclinations resurfaced. I was not going to stop him this time.

His lips found mine, moving softly. Jason pulled back with a lusty look in his eye. "One drink?"

"Okay," I breathed against his mouth, mesmerised by him. I missed those kisses.

He got out and opened the door for me, leading me by the hand up the stairs to his place. He was so charming as he poured us each a drink. Downing it, he poured more and playfully challenged me to a shot race, betting I couldn't chug all three faster than him. He was right, of course. I couldn't.

As the liquor soaked into my system, Jason took me on a tour of his apartment. It was a pretty impressive place, with a large sunken living room, gleaming kitchen, three bedrooms, and a balcony. One bedroom belonged to his roommate, who was away for the weekend. He winked, grinning. If he were a cartoon right then, I'm sure there would be a twinkling star on his teeth. The extra bedroom he used as his drafting room, the walls covered with plans and blueprints, a drawing table at one end. He was studying to become an architect with his father's firm and clearly *very* determined to follow in his notable footsteps. Jason's family was quite well off.

The last stop was his bedroom, filled with modern decor (well, modern for 1997), the style very chic. His bed was covered by a masculine grey comforter, sleek and silky-smooth. I assumed he must have a hired cleaner, as not many single men I knew cared about arranging throw pillows. He waved his arms grandly as we walked in, announcing, "This is where the magic happens." Never mind the room—his smile was magical.

"This is a real bachelor pad," I commented with a laugh. "A very impressive place."

"Thanks. Yeah, I guess it is a bit of a 'pad.' But I just haven't found the right girl yet. It needs a feminine touch, don't you think?" He slipped behind me, nuzzling my neck as his arms wrapped around my waist. I felt my heart flutter...and something else too. He spun me in his arms, his mouth falling onto mine, fingers wrapping in my hair. I was a bit surprised by the aggressive sexuality. Jason had always been a sweetheart without fail, so this was a whole new side of his personality.

"Whoa, let's not rush things," I took a step back. He looked irritated for a split second, but it vanished quickly. He held my hands, laughing at his own enthusiasm like an embarrassed schoolboy.

"I'm sorry. I am just so into you, Linda, I can't help myself. You are everything I've ever wanted in a woman." Jason stepped closer again, his eyes locking with mine as he caressed my cheek. "I am falling in love with you."

And there they were. The words I had wanted to hear again for twenty-two painful years. This was the man of my dreams, standing before my very eyes. Without a second thought, I threw myself into his arms, kissing him passionately. This deal was getting sealed tonight.

He had no idea what he was in for. I was going to rock his world.

THE MORNING CAME TOO SOON. A SOFT BILLOWY LIGHT cascaded in from the windows as I opened my eyes and ran a hand through my thoroughly dishevelled hair. Last night had been better than any daydream I'd ever had. Jason was a rocket in the sack, full of endless energy, and very enthusiastic. Almost overly so at times. He knew his way around a woman, I could tell, but most of his focus remained on his own pleasure. That was not uncommon in my experience. *We can work on that,* I thought with a smile. *It was our first night together, after all. There's plenty of time to work out the kinks.*

Where was that love of mine? Jason's side of the bed was empty. I crawled out from under the crumpled sheets, finding my clothing to get dressed. As I pulled on my skirt, I noticed something was very different about my right foot. *Holy shit!* I had a sixth toe. An extra little pinky toe stuck onto the end.

I wiggled it. Well, at least now I knew what my side effect was. I should have felt more horrified, but instead, I found myself thankful

I didn't have a third eye or a tennis ball in my butt cheek or something. I could handle a toe. *Plastic surgery, here I come.*

I peered out the bedroom door to see Jason sitting in a pedestal chair at the kitchen island, sipping on a coffee. He wore a dapper-looking outfit, suit pants and dress shirt, as if he was heading to a job interview.

"Good morning, handsome," I greeted with a smile, looking forward to a brand-new day.

"Good morning. Do you want some coffee for the road?" he turned his head and asked, returning a more polite smile.

"For the road?" I walked up and wrapped my arms around his chest from behind, kissing him on the cheek. "I thought maybe we could grab some breakfast."

"Oh man, I can't. My father called me into work. He wants me to sit in on an important meeting to learn the ropes." He slipped out of my arms and walked to the coffee pot. He filled up a *Styrofoam* go-cup, snapping a lid on top. *Who keeps go-cups in their apartment?*

"You disappeared on me this morning. I'd hoped for some morning cuddles." I winked, taking the cup he offered. I moved in for a kiss.

"Yeah," he stepped back, hands settling on his hips. "About that...listen. Last night was fun." He reached to grab his suit jacket draped over the back of the stool.

My smile faded, sensing something wasn't quite right. His temperature was cool as he regarded me, not his usual self at all.

"It was. Very much so," I agreed, brows raised, waiting for him to continue.

"But I just don't think *this*"—he waved his hand between us—"is working for me."

"What?" I was shocked and confused. My pulse pounded. "But you said you were falling in love with me last night."

How does a person flip their feelings so quickly? They don't.

"I say a lot of things to get what I want." He adjusted his cuffs and lapels, very business-like.

"So that was a lie? Was it all a lie?"

"You have this innocent farmgirl thing going on that I found irresistible. I just had to try a sample." His lips twitched, amused.

"Sample?" I was incredulous, an instant heat flaming my cheeks. *I'm some kind of bizarre conquest?* "But we've dated for months!"

"You're a tough nut to crack, admittedly. It took way more time and effort than I imagined."

"How dare you!" I flew at him and his smug little smirk. He grabbed my wrists and pushed me back. I stumbled but straightened myself right away, glaring at him.

Jason smoothed down his hair. "No need for theatrics. Men sleep with women; it's the way of the world. You didn't have to say yes last night. Own up to your own sexuality, will you?" He headed to the front door, tossing my jean jacket over to me.

"You're trying to put this back on *me*? You shouldn't have lied! Saying you loved me...you manipulated me, used me. I didn't sign up for that." I was so angry, I was shaking.

Jason shrugged. "Well, it went how it went. Can't go back now. There's no point in dwelling on things you can't change."

His words smacked me in the face. So callous and uncaring. Devoid of basic humanity or empathy. And devilishly ironic, given the situation.

I was finally seeing him for who—or what—he really was. His true colors. Jason wasn't the ungettable get or the key to a dreamy, pampered life. No, he was an asshole. An entitled rich boy, clearly living only for his own selfish adventures. *How did I not pick up on this before?* My mind spun. *Or maybe I did. I broke up with him twenty-two years ago, after all. Had I sensed something was off back then?*

"You have no idea what I've been through for you. You were the one that got away." I growled, "How stupid am I?"

Jason looked confused. "What are you talking about?" He shook his head, scoffing.

I was a different girl when this first happened, with big dreams and high moral fiber. Thinking back on it now, I clearly must've picked up on this slimy part of him. But why didn't I remember the specifics? *Perhaps I blocked it all out.* In my aging desperation, was it possible I let the torture of that unexplained 'what if' taint my logic over time?

He opened the door, motioning for me to walk through it. Another damn door. "Thanks for a pleasant evening. Take care," he said, straight-faced. I picked up my go-cup.

I was so mad at him but equally mad at myself. I actually walked through that damn quicksand door for this useless excuse for a man.

No point in dwelling on the things you can't change, he'd said. Begrudgingly, I admitted how right he'd been. That's exactly what I'd done for a large chunk of my life, dwelling on an unknown and letting it fester, boring a hole right through me. I'd let the experience rule me rather than shape me in moving forward.

"Come on, I need to leave soon." He waved faster, impatient.

I hurled my coffee at him with my dominant farmgirl throwing arm. Jason tried to dodge it but couldn't. I heard the lid pop off as it connected with his torso, brown liquid splashing down his shirt and pants. He squealed, feeling the heat. As the wet stain grew, soaking into the fibers of his no-doubt expensive outfit, a smile spread across my face. That felt slightly better.

"Oh no! I hope you're not *late*." I stomped past Jason, pushing him back against the door on my way by. He lashed out, clamping a hand onto my wrist, squeezing hard. He stared me down, his jaw flexing as his teeth clenched.

The intensity of his eyes jarred me.

"Let me go! Or would you like an assault charge to tarnish your daddy's image of you?" I matched his glare, deciding not to back down. I could tell he was fighting to contain his temper or whatever other urges existed there. Was he capable of worse?

Worry began to seep in just as his hand released me, fingers popping open as if spring-loaded, lowering to clench into a fist by his side. The look on his face was disturbing, dark. I spun on my heel and stalked briskly down the hall, getting the hell away from him. When I didn't hear footsteps behind me as I rushed down the stairs, my relief swelled. Reaching safety was my first priority, and then maybe having a stiff drink.

Once I was out of the building and standing on the sidewalk, out of the danger zone, I let out a huge breath, expelling the many uncomfortable emotions pent up inside my body. Both my head and my heart ached, my pulse still in the process of slowing.

Well, that didn't go the way I thought. No wonder he's still single 22 years from now. This is exactly why some people don't call Mr. Regret an angel, I mused, remembering his earlier comment. Doing a mistake over again didn't mean it was going to offer a better result. Sometimes, it turned out badly. *Like now.*

"So, I'm officially stuck here," I muttered to myself. "I have to live my useless old life all over again. Every shitty depressing part of it. No perfect man. No sunny future to look forward to." I sighed, staring down at my sixth toe, clad in a simple leather sandal. "And no *Jimmy Choo's.*"

But I'm young and skinny again, so there's that. I shrugged.

My body felt dirty, in much need of a shower. Knowing what I knew now, I figured that asshole's germs would easily glow beneath a blacklight. It was imperative I wash all traces of Jason from my body immediately.

I started walking toward my old apartment. Well, it wasn't so old anymore. In this timeline, I'd just moved in from the University residence last year. Nothing was past tense anymore. *I'm in it. This is now. Again.*

Tears welled in my eyes as the full weight of my error crashed down upon me. Furiously, I blinked the wetness away. "I should have just returned to the bridge."

But then a thought popped into my brain. *My life doesn't have to be as bad as before, does it?* I grudgingly acknowledged that I'd let a lot of crappy things occur, usually because I was stuck wallowing about the past, which cumulatively drove me to hopelessness. Couldn't I simply make better decisions from this point on? If I did that, all those things that plagued me before wouldn't afflict me now. Well, not all of them anyway.

I had closure on Jason, at least. An unfortunate kind, but closure nonetheless.

Why did I let the "what if's" drive me so crazy?

"That kind of thinking stops right now, Linda." I thrust out a stern fist, giving myself a serious pep talk.

Forcing myself to think positively was helping. I actually felt some hope. My mood continued to lighten, and I glanced at my surroundings with a whole new tint on the lens.

This turn of events didn't have to be horrible because I wouldn't *let* it be horrible. I now had the benefit of all my life experience to guide me.

Wait...

My eyes widened in sudden realisation.

23 45 98 12 72.

I dug a pen out of my purse and scribbled the numbers, just in case another random side effect decided to hit, and I lost my memory or something. I also jotted down the exact date I lost out on that damn work lottery. "Thank goodness I've always had a good mind for numbers."

A slow smile spread on my lips.

Maybe Mr. Regret was an angel after all.

JEREMIAH RABBIT

D avid was due to jog by any minute. Discreetly, I ensured the 'ladies' weren't escaping the low-cut neckline of my skin-tight, strapless dress. A lush flow of red hair cascaded over one shoulder, perfectly complementing my plump rouge lips. I'm not going to lie—my inspiration was totally Jessica Rabbit.

Countless masculine eyes perused my vivacious form as I struck a seductive pose, enhancing my generously conjured curves. The goal was to be noticed, so I guess it was working.

"This better be worth it," I muttered.

The outcome of my final exam hinged on my ability to train a novice wizard. Catch was, ancient wizarding rules forbade me from initiating contact with a potential apprentice. I couldn't just walk up and introduce myself or even wave. I despised the archaic rules, but in order to see my dream of earning Master Wizard status become reality, I had to follow them. Rebelling equalled automatic failure, and that simply wouldn't do.

The possibility of securing David as a pupil thrilled me. The man possessed a natural skill he didn't even realize, and miraculously, he hadn't been snatched up yet. However, he was also very handsome. My previous—and somewhat disastrous—dating experience dictated that my average-looking self had next-to-no chance of catching his eye. Guys like David went for well-dressed, cellulite-free beauties with nary a hair out of place. Thus, I had to become *irresistible*.

Cue Jessica Rabbit.

"Excuse me? I couldn't help but notice you standing there." A slick-haired man at least ten years my senior strolled up to my park bench. He wore a too-snug jogging suit with neon green stripes, and his hungry eyes slithered all over my 'assets.'

I groaned inwardly. "Can I help you?"

He pointed to a decorative zipper adorning my hip. "Actually, I wanted to ask if that's a mirror in your pocket? Because I can see myself getting into your skirt." Leaning in with a crooked grin, he purred, "Where have you been all my life?"

His breath smelled of eau de fried onions. I quickly tapped my fingers on the empty pocket in question, conjuring a hand-mirror.

"Oh, you mean this?" I feigned innocence, brandishing it with a flourish. "Why yes, it is. Good guess! However, I don't think we're seeing the same reflection." Cocking a brow, I flipped the mirror in my hand. Senior sleazeball's eyes widened as he saw his new and improved image, complete with a bloody nose, missing teeth, and black eye. "This is what happens to creepy losers who use lame pickup lines."

Aghast, his thick fingers flew to his perfectly unharmed face. Realising the deception, he scowled. "Whatever, you crazy bitch," he spat, before walking off in a huff.

"Mmm-kay, bye!" I gave a half-hearted wave.

The sound of rhythmic footfalls approached.

Oh, crap! Quickly re-striking my pose, I plumped up the ladies again, emanating a smouldering come-hither stare. David passed by the bench I had draped myself over moments later, and as expected, his glance inevitably slid my way. *Yes!*

He gave me a polite nod in return, not slowing in the slightest. *No!*

As I watched my quarry fade into the distance, I slumped down onto the bench. *What did I do wrong?* I stared after him, completely baffled, until something interesting caught my eye. David had just craned his neck to check out another jogger.

A male jogger.

"Of course!" My thoughts brightened with a whole new plan.

Wasting zero time, I vanished into the trees and raked my hands over my frame, head to toe. My curvy form shifted and glimmered beneath pulsating fingertips, and within seconds, had fully morphed into a hardened body. "Jessica Rabbit, meet *Jeremiah* Rabbit."

Teleporting to the other side of the park, I whispered, "I can still do this. I'll simply run back towards my car—and if I happen to cross paths with David along the way, so be it."

The target came into view much faster than expected, our trajectories converging within minutes. As David passed by for the second time, I flexed my rippling muscles and shot him the sexiest look I could muster. Our eyes met briefly, and then he was gone. *C'mon, c'mon...*

An agonising few seconds ticked by. Had I flubbed everything up again? Was I that bad a flirt? But when a flurry of shuffling footsteps rang out behind me, I swallowed a triumphant shout.

My future apprentice reappeared beside me; his smile bright. "Hi there."

Mission accomplished.

ECHO LAKE

Helen pressed her weathered lips against the slimy scales of a large pikanu fish. She leaned back, staring at the creature expectantly. But it only eyed her warily, its mouth opening and closing.

Nothing.

"Damn it, Clyde." Helen tossed the fish onto the ice. She clubbed it over the head with two brisk swings, watching its movement still. Four fish sat in her bucket now—only one more allowed. She didn't dare go over the daily catch limit.

Green Mother was always watching.

A northerly gust ruffled the dishevelled silver hair Helen's fur hat didn't cover. She watched as the air rolled across the snow-covered ice, colliding with the trees that slathered Echo Lake's gentle hills. She pulled a thick blanket over her shoulders and settled back onto her wooden stool. Dropping her hook into the depths below, Helen waited and hoped for her husband to take the bait, just as she'd done day in and day out for the last twenty-five years.

The townies had never believed her story. They said she'd lost her mind, never once taking a moment to truly listen. And as time passed, they began calling her crazy old Mrs. Finch...the fish kisser.

Especially the young ones. They were ruthless in their taunts. Helen knew the truth, though. Sure, she might be getting older, but her mind was still sharp.

They were ignorant, the lot of 'em, convinced that her beloved husband simply up and left. Chased off by her craziness. She'd heard the whispers, folks wondering why such a handsome man like Clyde chose to marry damaged stock like Helen. In their eyes, she'd been nothing more than a convenience for him, filling his bed and his belly until a better option presented itself.

Perhaps she'd been pretty enough in her younger years, but she'd simply never meshed with town life. Not only was she horribly awkward in social situations, but she'd also had to contend with her mother's tarnished reputation which loomed over her like a shadow. As soon as she was of age, she chose to move into the wild. Once there, she focused on her dream of living off the land and firing pottery in peace.

Then Clyde came along.

He'd stopped into her tiny workshop and bought one of her glazed bowls as a present for his mother. To her surprise, he'd stayed a while. Clyde was a skilled carpenter, strong of body, and always made her laugh. He adored Helen's creativity, enthralled by the fairy tales she loved to tell as she shaped formless hunks of clay into something beautiful. He kept coming back. Clearly, the man saw something special in her—enough to ignore all the naysayers.

Helen sighed into the lonely darkness that permeated Echo Lake. As she bobbed the hook up and down in the icy water, only the memories of Clyde kept her company now.

Her thoughts trailed back to when it happened, so long ago. Well, *the day before* it happened, to be exact. The Green Mother had arrived in their tiny community on a swirling breeze. Helen was in town for a few groceries that day and happened to witness the deity's cyclone settle in the village square. Like everyone else, she'd dropped everything to stare at the breathtaking goddess. A physical visit by the Green Mother had never happened before. Her decrees had always been heard, imparted by her powerful voice alone. She immediately captured everyone's attention.

Well, nearly everyone's.

Acting as Nature's right hand, the Green Mother impressed a warning upon every single soul present while her formless voice reached out to those who were not. "Echo Lake is not to be fished," she decreed as the air swept around her graceful, vine-covered frame. The light pooled within her violet irises, nearly outshining the sun. "You have depleted one of the lake's most precious resources. The fish need time to replenish."

Her words caused quite a stir, and everybody glanced about with wide eyes, clearly terrified of what else she might restrict. Echo Lake was one of the few water holes near the quaint northern town of Billowdale and a most reliable food source.

Green Mother continued, "Fear not, for you may fish the remaining lakes nearby, so long as you don't succumb to humanity's ingrained tendencies for excess. Five fish per day, per household, and no more." Audible sighs of relief rippled through the crowd. The deity finished by whispering into everyone's collective ears, "Any who ignore my decree shall stew on their transgressions within the lake. Heed my warning." With that, the breeze blew into a cyclone once more, and Green Mother was gone.

Helen recalled how the townspeople blinked furiously, shaking their heads and stumbling about in confusion after the goddess vanished. Everyone had clearly seen her, yet they couldn't remember it. They only recalled hearing her message, her decree, infused as law into their minds. Helen hadn't remembered seeing her then, either. *Not yet...*

Now Clyde, despite his many charms, was a stubborn man and hard of hearing since childhood—born that way. The very next day, he went to Echo Lake, and like always, he'd brought Helen along to keep him company. Clyde claimed he hadn't heard any whispered commands, but Helen couldn't fathom such a thing. How had he not heard the Green Mother's voice? Was his hearing loss to blame?

She tried to explain the decree, emphasising, "Nobody is to fish Echo Lake." But her husband wouldn't listen. He remained resolute that he'd never heard anything from this 'Green Mother' everyone worshipped and shouldn't have to follow any ridiculous rules laid down by some unknown *thing*.

"If I can't see it or hear it, it ain't real," Clyde stated with a firm nod.

Helen explained for the hundredth time, "But I swear to you, she's real. Everyone hears her!" It was mystifying how this wonderful man she'd fallen in love with could be so pig-headed.

"I do not believe in such naturalistic nonsense," Clyde scoffed. "Someone telling me where to fish. Whether I pull them out of this lake or another, makes no difference. They all go to the same place..." He made a show of patting his belly. "Besides, a husband's job is to keep his wife happy—and fed. Especially if we're going to start a family soon."

He gave her lips a peck. Wading into the water, Clyde grinned back at Helen, who sat nervously in her lawn chair along the shore. Normally she'd read a book and idly sip coffee in the sunshine but such relaxation seemed impossible this time. Her mind was far too preoccupied.

"Clyde, can you just fish somewhere else for a while? Please?" Helen begged.

With a wink, he cocked the rod over his shoulder. "It will be fine, my love."

Helen growled, getting irritated now. "Clyde, seriously, don't—"

The line arced through the air, cutting her off.

She still recalled the exact moment his hook hit the water. It replayed in her dreams on an endless loop, the time-worn images frayed and hazy at the edges. Before the hook's impact even perpetuated a ripple, she saw Clyde's body transform into a pikanu fish. His form contorted and shrunk in the space of a blink, his tail swishing in mid-air before dropping into the water with a *plop*.

Helen stared in horror as Clyde's clothing floated back to shore on the waves.

He was gone.

The wind swirled where her husband had vanished, growing into a torrential cyclone. The glistening image of a face manifested in the whipping liquid—one adorned with vines and flowers. In an instant, memory rushed back to Helen. She remembered seeing the Green Mother with vivid clarity in the square the day before. The voice Clyde swore he'd never heard before spoke solemnly, each word emanating from everywhere at once. "My warning was given and ignored. Punishment is now given. And so shall it be."

The fluid image of the Goddess thinned as the cyclone began to dissipate.

"Green Mother, don't go! Please have mercy on my husband! He didn't know!"

The deity nodded indifferently as her visage disintegrated into a fine spray of droplets. "What is done, is done." In the next moment, she disappeared, the remaining mist whisked across the lake.

"No! Please!" Helen cried, lunging into the water with arms outstretched. But it was no use.

The Green Mother was gone.

From that moment on, she became obsessed with finding her husband. He was still alive in that lake somewhere—she was sure of it—and she had to get him back. Helen pleaded with the townspeople to help, explaining what transpired, but nobody paid her any mind. They believed any claim to *see* the Goddess was simply too fantastical. Helen was likened to her late mother telling stories about meeting Green Mother, and they accused her of the same delusion.

Helen grew frustrated. They still couldn't recall seeing Green Mother in the town square. For some unknown reason, only she'd been given the gift of clarity—though it felt more like a curse.

Their closed mindedness was heartbreaking but sadly not a surprise.

Unwilling to give up, Helen gathered the supplies her mother taught her about as a young girl. She'd held numerous rituals, chanting repeatedly and calling out in desperation for Nature's right hand to return. However, when the great Green Mother finally did acknowledge her efforts and granted Helen an audience, the Goddess maintained the punishment fit the crime.

Dismayed and left with no other choice, Helen was forced to wait until Green Mother lifted the fishing ban on Echo Lake. Two years of waiting followed, and it felt like a lifetime had passed her by. But finally, she stood in her husband's favourite fishing spot once again, rod in hand. She was determined to find Clyde, even if it meant catching every single fish in the lake.

Unfortunately, she wasn't alone...

With the ban lifted, others had shown up to fish Echo Lake, too. Fear tremored within as she realized any pikanu pulled from those cool waters could be her husband—a stark and terrible reality Helen couldn't abide.

The fishing pole jerked in her hands, jarring Helen from her tumultuous memories. Dispelling the twenty-year-old recollections from her mind, she furiously reeled in the line, leaning back. Air bubbles broke the surface seconds before a monstrous pikanu emerged from the icy hole. It was black as pitch with jagged scars snaking all over its body. This old fish had clearly been through many a fight in its day.

Helen hoisted the heavy creature with a groan, struggling to keep her grip. Closing her eyes, she centred every shred of focus onto the desperate love she held within her heart. Then she pressed her lips against a set of slimy scales for the fifth time that day.

From an early age, her mother had imparted the wisdom that every single fairytale blossomed from true beginnings. Helen had long since believed in that concept and now latched on to it. It was the fuel that continued motivating her. She grasped at hope, kissing every single pikanu fish she caught, for if the power of true love's kiss could break spells in fairy tales, why shouldn't it break the magic holding Clyde captive?

As time passed, she considered giving it up—all of it. Yet, Helen could never bring herself to do it. Perhaps some of Clyde's stubbornness rubbed off on her.

The pikanu in her hands stared back at her with blank eyes. No response.

Releasing a defeated sigh, Helen tossed the fish onto the ice and reached for her billy club. That made five—her catch limit for the day. "Sorry, old guy. But I can't put you back. If I did that, I'd never find my Clyde."

But before she could strike, a stiff wind kicked up, swirling snowflakes around her in oddly sweeping curls. It carried the sound of youthful giggles to her ears, staying her hand. Helen's eyes snapped to the shoreline, spying two young boys there. She dropped the club, frowning. Hardly anybody dared to bother her here anymore except for youngsters who still found some measure of thrill watching the *fish kisser*.

For over twenty years, she'd been scaring townies off the shores of Echo Lake. All of them, by any means. Since nobody took her seriously, and since Helen couldn't risk anyone else catching Clyde, she'd resorted to drastic measures. After slathering her skin with pungent oils, she'd worn ragged fabrics and furs to appear animalistic, then growled, screamed, and waved sharpened sticks to frighten off whoever dared approach the water's edge.

However, when her antics landed her in Billowdale's lockup, leaving Clyde vulnerable for too many nights in a row, she finally realized what needed to be done. In order to protect her beloved from would-be husband killers, she gathered all of their life savings together and leased the land surrounding Echo Lake. Not an easy task, but one she completed.

As she trudged toward the shoreline, Helen wagged a crooked finger at the boys. "You kids get off my property! This isn't some freakshow. Go away!"

The boys ignored her and belly-laughed a moment longer before their expressions abruptly sobered. Their arms lifted; fingers pointed at Helen. The children's eyes grew round as buttons.

She cackled. "That's right, you little ruffians. You *should* be scared! Now, get out of here! Run in fear from crazy old Mrs. Finch!"

But the boys continued pointing, their urgency intensifying until they leapt off the ground. "Look! Behind you!" they finally screamed.

A pit of dread dug deep into Helen's stomach. Had a predator ventured out onto the frozen lake in search of an easy meal?

Fighting her fear, she glanced over her shoulder, then shuffled back in alarm. A man appeared on the ice before her with scraggly grey hair and a dishevelled beard...as naked as a newborn. His skin glistened with moisture in the muted light, his body covered with jagged scars. *Just like the fish.* She glanced down, confirming her grisly catch had vanished.

"Helen..." the man murmured. The wind kicked up again, those same odd curls billowing all around him.

She stilled, her heart leaping in her chest. *That voice...could it be?*

"It's me—Clyde." The man opened his arms, a broad grin barely visible beneath his hair.

"C-Clyde?" Helen stuttered as she stepped closer. She searched the depths of the man's hooded emerald eyes and tears welled up from within her, quickly overflowing. "Clyde!"

"The one and only. I've missed you, my love." His arms spread wider.

"Oh, I found you!" She rushed to him, shuddering to think that she'd nearly clubbed him to death only moments before. If it hadn't been for those boys' voices carried on the breeze, things would've been tragically different.

The breeze, she thought, recalling how it had kicked up in random gusts, showcasing those odd whorls. Had Green Mother been present? Had she finally taken pity on them after all these years?

"I can't believe I finally found you!" she cried. Clyde swept her into his arms, bending to kiss her lips. The man reeked of lake water and fish, but Helen didn't care. He was back.

She pulled away, her clothes slick with slime, and quickly retrieved her blanket to warm him up. But when she turned back around, instead of finding her beloved, Helen peered down at the scarred old fish flopping on the ice again. And it slid dangerously close to the hole.

"No!" Helen lunged forward with arms outstretched, her nails digging into the slippery pikanu tail just before fish-Clyde dipped into the slushy hole. Quickly, she flung him away from the edge.

Ignoring the still-gawking kids, Helen scurried to secure her husband and kissed his scaley head once more. She suddenly felt happy to have witnesses. All those good-for-nothing townies would have to eat plenty of crow once word got out about this.

Clyde's black, torpedo-shaped body shuddered within her grasp, twisting and morphing until he became himself again. He rubbed at fresh pink scratches on his buttocks where Helen's nails had dug in, the scales and thrashing tail long gone.

"Oh, my goodness!" Helen exclaimed. "I worried I'd lost you twice!" Helen latched onto him, and the pair kissed passionately. However, after several moments his lips disappeared, and the blanket fell limp in her arms once more.

What the...?

Frazzled, Helen collected her fish-husband and rushed toward her tiny cabin nestled at the edge of the lake. She took him indoors, proceeding to kiss fish-Clyde over and over. Every single time, he appeared in full form. But then, after a few moments passed, he turned back into a fish.

"What do we do?" Helen fretted after a fresh kiss.

Her husband sighed and wrapped a strong arm around her shoulders, squeezing reassuringly. "We will figure this out. Don't worr—" Clyde's words halted as he shrunk, flopping back to the floor.

Helen groaned, swiftly sweeping him up and kissing him back into proper shape. "I'll appeal to Green Mother straight away! But what if she won't listen?"

Clyde shrugged, a playful grin spreading across his raggedy features. "I guess I'll be needing a fish tank then." He pulled his wife close, a familiar twinkle gleaming in his eye. "And you'll need some lip balm." His face lowered toward hers.

Helen pulled back, slapping his shoulder, "This is serious! No time for jokes." Though, deep down, she loved hearing his one-liners again. It was worth it to see him grin at her like that.

Clyde's face twitched oddly, then collapsed in on itself. His shoulders and torso followed suit, and Helen scrambled to catch his diminishing body as it fell yet again.

"For goodness' sake." After giving him a quick peck, Helen set Clyde down and rushed through an adjoining door into her workshop storage room, sidestepping stacks of pottery. As she dug frantically into the corner, she heard the sound of bare footsteps approach from behind.

"Wow. These are beautiful," Clyde said, bending to inspect several glazed mugs sitting on a wooden shelf.

"Thank you," she replied, shoving a box out of the way. "Pottery has helped keep me sane. *Ah ha!* There it is!" Helen emerged victorious, turning with a large washing tub in hand.

But her husband was flopping again.

Growling, Helen bent her achy knees and kissed his cheek, then rushed to fill the tub with water. They certainly couldn't continue like this forever. They just couldn't.

"I take it that's for me," Clyde said a moment later, rejoining her in the kitchen. His steady hand squeezed her shoulder, and he flashed the charming smile she'd missed so much. Helen's heart flip-flopped in her chest.

"It is." Helen nodded. "You'll need a safe place to be while I work and sleep. It's only until we can figure this out, my love."

"I understa—"

With a sigh, Helen gently submerged fish-Clyde into the cool water, shifting the basin nearer to the fireplace for warmth. "It will be dark soon, and there are chores to be done before bed." Looking down at him, knowing her eyes likely betrayed her emotions, Helen felt horrible having to leave him there...yet, she couldn't possibly complete her daily tasks while stopping to kiss him every couple of minutes. "You'll need to stay in there for a little while."

A single bubble flittered to the surface as fish-Clyde opened and closed his pointy u-shaped mouth. She took that as his assent.

"I'll be back soon."

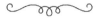

Two days passed.

The setting sun painted the sky with tangerine and fuchsia strokes as Helen settled into her new nightly routine. She stoked the flames in the stone fireplace, sprinkling the flickering heat with Calinia, a special mixture of semba seeds and dried pareema petals she'd harvested and preserved during the summer months. It was a sacred concoction passed down through generations, shared with Helen by her mother, and the only known way to open a channel to Green Mother.

A rich and tangy aroma permeated every corner of her rustic home. *Their* rustic home Helen reminded herself. She wasn't alone anymore.

Clyde watched on from his basin as Helen chanted. Thus far, the Green Mother had ignored her calls. But Helen truly believed the deity was present within the wind that day she pulled Clyde from the ice, a belief that spurred her to continue trying. The Green Mother couldn't be so cruel as to leave them in this situation, could she? Hadn't they paid their penance by now?

Nearly twenty minutes passed with nothing but the steady crackling of the wood to show for her efforts. Helen ceased chanting and looked down at her husband, her hopes waning. "My Calinia supply is dwindling, Clyde. If she doesn't come soon, we might be out of luck until summer."

She lifted him from the water for a kiss, wiping moisture from her eyes as he materialised. "What will we do?"

Clyde wrapped her up in his arms, letting out a long sigh. "Well, at least I'm used to being a fish. You can leave me in the basin as long as you need to each day, okay? You can't be wearing out your muscles hauling me around everywhere." He leaned the side of his head against hers.

"Oh, Clyde..." Helen's voice shook.

As her husband quietly shrunk beside her, the wind kicked up outside, rattling the loose cedar siding boards she kept forgetting to fix. Within the time it took for her to place her husband safely back into his basin, the gusts howled.

"A storm must be rolling in. I should go shutter the windows." Helen stood but didn't get far.

The front door swung wide, slamming against the wall in a torrent of swirling air that nearly flattened the flames in the fireplace. Helen's hair flew about her face, her mouth hanging agape, as she watched the effervescent visage of Green Mother float inside.

The door slammed shut behind her, and the cyclonic air calmed to a light breeze.

Green Mother looked just as she had twenty-five years before. Leafy vines slithered around the Goddess's slender, olive-tinged limbs. A high-necked dress of local and tropical flora layered her shimmering form—home to a kaleidoscope of colourful flowers that glowed from within. Her wide and knowing eyes shone a cool violet as they regarded Helen.

"You're really here..." Helen mumbled, then broke free of her shock, tilting her head in respect. "You bless me with your presence, Green Mother. Thank you for hearing my calls." If only the townspeople could see this, too—undeniable proof she wasn't crazy.

The deity nodded. "For what reason have you sought an audience with me?"

Helen swallowed hard. "Green Mother, many years ago my husband defied your decree not to fish on Echo Lake and was turned into a pikanu as punishment for his crime."

"I remember. What of it?" The Mother's delicate brows rose ever so slightly.

Helen pointed to the tub, her husband's tail thrashing within. "That day, when he went into the water, I thought I'd lost him forever—lost everything. But I finally found him. The old fairy tales are real, you see? It was my kiss that brought him back somehow!"

"A kiss...yes, yes." The Green Mother's lips twitched, teasing a smile that never arrived. "Such a mark of true love is one of the few forces powerful enough to weaken my magics." Emerald light flared in her palms as her fingers rippled like windblown wildflowers.

It only weakens her magic.

"Green Mother, I humbly plead with you to release Clyde from his punishment. It has been many years and surely you must know he has learned his lesson. And—" Helen's voice cracked, and she paused to pull in a breath. "I, too, have paid for his crime, living a life of ridicule. Of heartbreak, and loneliness."

Helen refused to look down at Clyde, knowing he could hear

every word. She took another deep breath, bolstering her courage. "As I fought to preserve my husband from being hooked by fishermen all these years, I *also* served you as a fierce protector of this lake."

Green Mother nodded, glancing down at Clyde, then back again. "Rest assured I have borne witness to your toil, Helen." A small smile finally spread on the Green Mother's face.

A seed of hope formed roots within her, and Helen capitalised on the opportunity. "Please, Green Mother. I'll do anything to have my husband back. I shall guard this place for the rest of my days. Be at your beck and call. Clyde won't put another hook in this lake ever again!" She sank to her knees, swallowing the twinge of arthritic pain it caused, and raised her hands. "Anything."

Green Mother's gaze softened. "You say Clyde has learned his lesson after all these years. Shall he speak for himself on the matter?" She motioned to the tub, her graceful fingers beckoning the large pikanu to rise.

Helen's breath quickened as Clyde's dripping feet formed and stepped out of the tub. Oh, how she couldn't wait to pitch that wretched water into the snowbank. Clyde rolled his head atop his neck, and bones cracked as he stretched his arms, stiff from being compressed into fish form.

Green Mother coughed discreetly, flicking a lithe wrist toward his bare lower regions.

"Oh!" Clyde snatched a blanket draped over the chair. Once his essentials were back under wraps, he flashed a charming smile. "My wife is right. I won't disobey you again now that I know you're real. I apologise for my ignorance. Back then, I had no idea and just thought all the Green Mother talk was nonsense. I couldn't hear—"

"Nonsense..." The goddess's eyes darkened as she cut off his words. Thorns sprouted from the vines circling her limbs. "I am nature's right hand, an advocate and keeper of this world's delicate balance. I am the *only* thing keeping you selfish people from destroying every precious, life-sustaining resource you take for granted." Her irises turned to embers amidst a swell of increasingly turbulent air. "And you thought I was *nonsense?*"

Helen waved her hands, shooting a glare at her husband. "Goodness no, Green Mother. You are powerful and wise." *And merciful,* she hoped. "Clyde knows this now. He believes. I assure you. He's just a little hard of hearing, you see, and for some reason, that kept him from comprehending you before."

Clyde's usual confidence had withered, his shoulders slumped. He bowed his head respectfully, almost sheepishly—something Helen had never seen before.

Green Mother's gaze slid back to the offender on trial, her words clipped. "What say you, Clyde? Are you now a believer?"

Clyde nodded. "Yes, your Excellency."

"Green Mother," she corrected sharply, turning away from them both.

"I'm sorry. Yes, Green Mother." Clyde met Helen's nervous gaze.

Time seemed to stop as the pair awaited the decision, their future together hanging in the balance. The Goddess paced back and forth, periodically glancing their way while she contemplated her course of action.

Finally, after several agonising minutes passed, Green Mother faced them again. "If it was up to me alone, I'd put you back in the lake," she told Clyde. "However, I've conferred with Nature and acknowledged people have proven they have the capacity to change —*if they choose to.*"

She looked at Helen. "You may have your husband back, provided you *both* continue to preserve this lake. Nature quite likes the idea of keeping this sanctuary intact. To maintain a place where flora and fauna can be at peace, relatively undisturbed."

Helen beamed. "Oh yes, of course! We'd be honoured to."

The light returned to her husband's eyes, his expression brightening. "Thank yo—"

"But before you thank me," the Goddess interrupted him again, raising a hand, "there is more. Clyde, you must vow to never drop a hook into water again. A violation will return you to the lake with no chance of pardon."

Without hesitation, Clyde stood tall and laid a hand over his heart. "I vow to never fish Echo Lake ever again."

Helen nodded enthusiastically. A note of hope thrummed within. Even if she had to wrestle the pole from his hands herself, she'd make sure he upheld that vow.

However, Green Mother shook her head, her eyes locked on Clyde. "No. Not just Echo Lake. *All* lakes."

Clyde faltered, clearing his throat loudly before he spoke. "Green Mother, with all due respect, a man must provide for his family. Will you grant me just one lake to fish? I will abide by the limit at all times."

"I will not. Your wife is quite capable of fishing for sustenance, and as compensation for her dedication, I will allow her to continue catching the daily limit on Echo Lake. *Only her.*" Green Mother gave a brisk nod. "That is my decision."

Overcome with relief, Helen beamed. What a wonderful outcome. "Oh, yes, we understand. Thank you for your kindness."

"Do you vow?"

Clyde shifted from one foot to the other. "May I have a moment with my wife, please?"

The deity's eyes flashed, but she agreed.

Helen stared in confusion at Clyde as he led her into the bedroom. He closed the door with a *click*, but before he could turn around, she'd already smacked him on the arm. "What are you doing?"

Clyde ran a hand through his wet hair. "She has forbidden me from fishing—forever. How can I not fish, Helen? That is what I do. What I've always done. A man fishes."

"Yes...as do women." Helen rested a hand on his forearm. "Rest assured, I've been fishing and trapping all the years you've been gone and got along just fine. It matters little to me who does the fishing as long as the fish get caught."

"But it matters to me!" His arms flew out to the side. "I can't sit idly by and let you do all the work. You've had to do that for too long, and it just isn't right. A husband takes care of his wife. My father was a useless, sorry excuse for a man. He barely lifted a finger to help his family thrive, and I refuse to be like him. I—" He stopped with a heavy sigh. Looking down, he inspected the many scars covering his skin, stark reminders of his time spent in Echo Lake.

Helen knew how deeply his father's shortcomings had affected Clyde, but surely, he had to recognize this circumstance was exceptional. She counted on her fingers, listing all the other kinds of work to be done. "See, there are plenty of ways to be useful." Then her voice broke, chin quivering. "But most importantly, you can *be here*. With me." A tear slid down her cheek.

Clyde's eyes softened. His head tilted, and his shoulders deflated. "Oh, Helen..."

"Isn't that what you want?" Her voice was a shaky whisper. When he didn't answer right away, her cheeks grew hot. "Or is your damn pride more important to you?" Clyde reached out for her, but she brushed his hand away.

The wind blew against the door, rattling the hinges. Green Mother grew impatient.

They stared at each other in silence.

Clyde's jaw clenched and brows pinched together, expression unreadable. At least before, he used to speak his mind whenever he didn't agree with her. The fact that he wasn't talking now felt foreign and unsettling. She didn't know what to make of it.

Helen wiped the moisture from her face. "Clyde? What are you thinking?"

The door rattled again, more forcefully this time.

Abruptly, he opened it and strode out to rejoin a very unimpressed looking Green Mother. Her eyes narrowed into thin slits as he approached.

Helen rushed after him, sliding to a stop by his side. She willed for her husband to meet her gaze, to send her a silent message that everything would be okay, but he didn't. *He's going to choose the lake. He won't face me because it's too hard.* A dull ache settled deep in her chest.

Had the townspeople been right all along—that he'd only married her to keep his bed and belly full? Had she fought all these years to free a man who never truly loved her? The caustic realisation of that was simply too great, and she had to sit down.

Clyde took a deep breath, straightened his shoulders, then thrust a pointed finger toward Helen. "Green Mother, I love this fine woman with all of my heart. The last twenty-five years have been terrible without her. My stubborn stupidity is what got us into this mess, and now I need to make it right. I will do whatever it takes."

Helen let out a shaky sob of relief. Her vision blurred with tears as she smiled, the weathered skin framing her mouth compressing like an accordion.

Clyde finally met Helen's gaze. "Do you know how I got all these scars?" He pointed to the various markings littering his body. "I kept swimming to the surface looking for you, fighting with larger fish every time. It's funny how a person doesn't fully realize what they have until they lose it." He helped her stand, circling a steadying arm about her waist. "I'm so sorry for not listening to you that day. For leaving you all alone. For everything."

"Oh, Clyde." She buried her face in his chest. He really *did* love her.

The shade of Green Mother's eyes had lightened during Clyde's speech, now glowing a brilliant pink. Her thorns retracted, hands coming to rest palm against palm in front of her chest. "I believe your words are genuine, Clyde. Now, once more I shall ask...do you vow?"

"Yes ma'am, I vow."

Her hands raised and lit with ethereal flame once more. Refulgent wisps poured from her fingertips, wafting across the room towards Clyde. He stiffened as fiery light danced around his body. Then, one by one, the wisps turned black and dissipated.

His skin glistened afterward, and he let out a bark of laughter. "It kind of tickles."

Helen clapped her hands with delight.

Green Mother's flowers were in full bloom by the time she lowered her hands. The last of the wisps evaporated, and a warm smile crossed her face. "And so, it shall be."

Clyde and Helen embraced as the air swirled about the room once more. The couple turned back to the Goddess who stood regally within the heart of the thickening funnel.

"Words can't express how thankful we are," Clyde said, that charming smile back on his face. "I promise we will take good care of Echo Lake."

The Goddess nodded. "I trust you shall." She levelled one last look at Clyde—a warning for him to keep his promise before turning away. "Now, I must take my leave. Nature calls." The front door swung open in a bluster of cyclonic flurries, snowflakes melting in awe of her radiance.

Helen leaned into her husband for support as their clothes whipped against their skin.

The goddess glanced back. "Be well." And with that, she vanished.

The door slammed shut, and silence befell their now dishevelled living room. Against the wall, the windblown fireplace struggled to regain its heat. And yet again...Clyde was naked. His hastily tied blanket had proved useless against such voracious gusts.

An unconcerned Clyde located the shroud hanging haphazardly from a lamp in the corner of the living area and grinned as he covered back up. "I'll need to get used to wearing clothes again."

Helen smirked, stepping up to the heavy tub of water she'd grown to despise. "Well, at least you won't be needing *this* anymore." She kicked the basin, letting loose a gleeful cackle as Clyde walked back to her side. Her beloved was finally whole and home to stay.

"Thankfully, no. *But* my love..." Clyde whisked Helen into his arms, dipping her as low as his ageing back dared. Her husband's mouth hovered above hers, and despite his dire need of a bath, his closeness riled the dormant butterflies stagnating within her stomach.

"Yes?" Helen replied, feeling breathless.

"We're still going to need that lip balm."

A NOT SO SILENT NIGHT

A DIALOGUE-ONLY STORY.

"Don't you think you've had enough cocoa for one evening, Nick?"

"There's *never* enough cocoa."

"But you've already had three."

"And I'll likely have a fourth too."

"For the love of snow, your drinking habits are getting a little out of hand."

"You eat your cookies; I drink my cocoa. We all have our vices."

"Really? You can't possibly believe those two things are equivalent."

"How many cookies do you bake in a day? What, maybe twenty-four dozen?"

"I *do* have to feed a lot of mouths up here."

"Well, *I* only eat *three* of those cookies. I know twenty-two dozen go out to the elves...so, where do the rest go? Straight to your hips."

"Oh, shut up."

"I'm just calling a spade a spade, Carol."

"As if you're one to talk! You are no GQ model either. Have you ever had a six-pack? Nope. Your gut's a *keg!*"

"Listen, I make shaking my belly like a bowl full of jelly look good."

"You're a horrible drunk, Nick."

"My flavoured liqueur says otherwise."

"Yeah, well, I'm pouring your *precious* liqueur down the sink."

"Hey, come back here!"

"Mmm? What was that? I can't hear you."

"Yes, you can. Don't you dare..."

"Oh?"

"Don't touch that bottle, woman!"

"What bottle are you referring to? *This* bottle?"

"Put. It. Down. I'm not going to say it again."

"Oooh, the big man has put his foot down. What will you do? Ho Ho Ho me to death?"

"Well Carol, you got the *ho* part right."

"Wha—now, what exactly do you mean by that?"

"Don't pretend to think I don't know. Standing there, acting all innocent."

"You're talking nonsense now. You should just go to bed and sleep it off."

"I'll go to bed when I'm darn good and ready to! And I'm not ready. I'm sick of you mothering me. I can do what I want."

"Oh, I am *well aware* that you don't need me for anything anymore, Nick."

"And now here comes the guilt trip. Perfect!"

"Okay, okay...just take a breath. Relax. Your whole face has turned red."

"Don't patronize me. What? Why are you looking at me like that?"

"I've had enough of this."

"No, don't pour out—"

"You are officially...cut OFF."

"Argh...Sweet Blitzen. Carol!"

"There! Put that in your pipe and smoke it. Thought I wouldn't actually do it, didn't ya?"

"You are pure evil."

"Yeah, well, you ain't no saint yourself."

"Technically, I am."

"Ugh, you just have to get the last word in. What has happened to you? You used to be so jolly. Kind and patient...and funny. Someone the elves could really look up to. Where's that loving man I married?"

"Things change after 1000 years of marriage. We've both changed."

"I can't argue that. But why is it we can't change together? All we ever seem to do is fight these last hundred years."

"Since December 24th, 1920 to be exact."

"Oh? And what is the significance of that date?"

"You know, Carol."

"You're looking at me funny right now. No, I *don't* know. Please explain."

"Why can't you just admit it? You had an affair."

"What? I did not."

"I was slaving away, prepping the sleigh, and coordinating the gift schedule. You knew I wouldn't be home for hours. On one of my *busiest* nights of the year, you were here...with Jimmy the cobbler. In our bed!"

"I—"

"Don't you dare deny it."

"Nick, you're drunk..."

"I'm buzzed; there's a difference. Don't change the subject. You've been caught with your hand in the cookie jar. I have proof!"

"Proof?"

"I suspected something was going on. So, I told the reindeer to keep an eye on you. But you were too busy riding cowboy to notice little ol' Rudolf shining his nose so bright at the window, weren't ya? He saw you plain as day."

"Look, Nick, it meant nothing..."

"You didn't even bother to close the curtains."

"Just let me explain—"

"Boy, I hope it was worth it. Sucking on a tiny elvish *lollipop*."

"Well, what did you expect? You were hardly ever around!"

"I'm Santa Claus, for fudge sake. I have duties and obligations. You knew what you were signing up for when you married me."

"Just sit down before you fall over. My goodness. I didn't sign up for being lonely and ignored. We haven't had a date night in over 300 years! And whenever there *was* time for us to be intimate, by some small miracle, you were always too tired. Or too busy stroking your gingerbread in the bathroom. Yah, I found your stash of nudie pictures hidden in the toilet tank, so carefully sealed in a *Ziploc*."

"Oh, ah…but I only ever thought of *you!*"

"Spare me the excuses. Not like your gingerbread works these days anyway."

"Wait—what was that?"

"Nothing."

"No, you just muttered something. What did you say?"

"Nothing. Just drop it."

"You said my gingerbread doesn't work."

"Oh, so you *did* hear me. Then why did you bother asking?"

"That's a low blow, Carol. The doctor said it's because I've been under a lot of stress. It has nothing to do with my advanced age. It's more common among men than people think."

"Well, common or not, women have needs too. *I have needs.*"

"Wow."

"Yeah, wow."

"I wish you would've talked to me before letting Jimmy frost your cookies."

"And I wish you would've made me feel like I *could*. You never listen to me."

"So, where does this leave us?"

"I don't know anymore, Nick. It feels like too much has happened. There's too much to overcome."

"Are you saying you want to throw in the towel?"

"Don't you? I'm tired of keeping up this charade for the sake of the elves. I cheated on you for goodness sakes, and you're practically an alcoholic. We live entirely separate lives. Our marriage hasn't been good for decades."

"No, it hasn't. I realize that. But has it really been 300 years since we've had a date night?"

"300 *long* years."

"Huh. I guess time has slipped away from me."

"A lot of things have slipped away from you, Nick."

"Okay, I get it. You can stop pointing at yourself. I suppose I have been a bit distant."

"A bit?"

"Just give me a minute to process everything."

"I'm going to bed."

"Carol, wait. I'm realizing now that I wasn't the best husband I could've been. The husband I *should've* been. Golly, that's hard to admit."

"You're not in your right mind. You'll feel differently in the morning, I'm sure."

"I may be a little tipsy, but I'm not stupid. I know my own thoughts."

"And here we go again..."

"No, Carol—no more fighting tonight. I swear."

"Fine. Whatever."

"Maybe we should just talk this all out. Clear the air. Calm and rational."

"It's not a good time to talk. I'm tired."

"Fine, then just listen. Look, I'm sorry."

"Wow. I can count on one hand how many times you've said those words to me."

"I was way more focused on being Santa than on being Nick. *Your* Nick."

"Do you really mean that? Or is it the booze talking?"

"I do."

"Well, then...I'm sorry too. I didn't mean to hurt you. I've felt horrible ever since."

"Thank you for that. I think it's good we're opening up like this finally. As hard as it is, these things really need to get hashed out."

"Yes, it's a start. But I don't know if it's enough, Nick."

"Not enough? So, you were serious about throwing in the towel?"

"I don't know what I feel right now. It's too much to process."

"Should we try couples' counselling?"

"And broadcast our marriage troubles across the Fablesphere? No thanks."

"Yeah, perhaps not."

"Can you imagine the rumour mill? You know how much of a gossip Jack Frost is. I shudder at the thought."

"Everybody will find out eventually when we divorce."

"*IF* we divorce."

"Aha! So, you *don't* want to throw in the towel! I knew it."

"Oh, Nick..."

"Why don't we just start slow by scheduling a date night?"

"I don't know. A lot of things need to change—starting with your cocoa problem."

"I'm not an alcoholic, Carol."

"When was the last day you remember *not* having a drink?"

"Uh...um, well...I'm not quite sure what to say."

"Then don't say anything. It's late. We should get to bed, anyway. Tomorrow's a big day—officially twelve days 'til Christmas. I have a lot of baking to do in the morning."

"Yeah, I suppose we should."

"I'd prefer you slept on the couch tonight. I need some space to think."

"Yeah, the couch is fine."

"Goodnight."

"Goodnight...argh. Carol, wait."

"What?"

"Listen, are you and Jimmy still...you know...together?"

"Goodness, no. It was only for a short time. I thought it might fill the void I felt inside, but I was very wrong. It turns out 'tiny elvish popsicle' as you called it, truly doesn't compare to Santa sausage."

"Santa sausage. Ha. That's cute."

"Okay, well...sleep tight."

"Hey, when did you get that nightie? I've never seen it before."

"On one of the many days you weren't here, husband. Shopping sometimes makes me feel better."

"Another way to fill the void?"

"Yes, but it never lasts. Nothing ever lasts."

"Well, it looks nice on you."

"Thanks. Now goodnight."

"Carol, I will quit drinking cocoa! Well, the liqueur kind anyway."

"Pshh. Right."

"No, really! Don't roll your eyes like that. I will. I promise."

"We should sleep on it. Let's talk again tomorrow with clear heads."

"No, not tomorrow. And what if I got the gingerbread working again? Would that help?"

"Of course, that would be wonderful, but I don't think it's an overnight fix, Nick."

"Actually, I think it might be. Look."

"Oh, my!"

"I've got my North Pole back!"

"I see that."

"You look beautiful tonight, you know. Hair curlers and all."

"Easy there, tiger."

"But why, sugar plum? Maybe this is what we've been missing! A good ol' roll in the hay."

"That's not a magical cure."

"No, but why not ease the tension while we work on everything else?"

"Well..."

"Give me your hands. Just think about it. I think *this* is what my gingerbread needed to get working all along. This talk. Release. Clarity. It's what *we* needed."

"You feel warm. Perhaps you have a fever."

"No, no. I'm fine. I'm thinking more clearly than I have in years. And it's *not the cocoa.*"

"Okay. I'm listening."

"We've hurt each other—badly. We hid it, ignored it. Let it sit and fester until it burned a hole right through our relationship. Do you agree?"

"I won't argue that point. We both have things to be sorry for."

"But we never talked about it. Golly, I wish I'd known the *real* reason you ran to Jimmy. I thought you were just being a heartless ice queen. And as time went on, I believed the booze could make it all disappear. But it didn't, of course."

"I tried to talk to you, Nick. Years ago. You kept ignoring me, so I gave up."

"Carol, I didn't listen, and I'm sorry. I was a real nincompoop."

"You put everything and everyone else before me. Why?"

"I was worried about letting the entire world down. There's so much pressure. Billions of children rely on me every year. A tiny mistake can wreck an entire childhood or kill the simple joy of believing in Santa. It consumed me."

"I can only imagine. That's something I wish you would've told me."

"I wish I had, too. And that was only part of it. When the ol' sleigh couldn't fly, so to speak, you have no idea how much it bothered me. Knowing I couldn't make you happy killed me inside."

"I didn't know it troubled you so much. You never showed it."

"I was stupid. It seemed easier to shut it off than face it. I pushed it all down and buried myself in work when I should've just leaned on you—my wife."

"After 1000 years of marriage, you finally realize this?"

"Better late than never. There. Now all our cards on the table."

"I don't think I've ever seen you like this. What's come over you?"

"A reality check. Sugar cake, I don't want to throw in the towel."

"Oh, Nick..."

"We both made mistakes. I know we can't go back, but we can go forward. I can forgive you, Carol, if you can forgive me. Can we give it another try? 1000 years is too much to flush down the drain. I still love you."

"You don't know what it means to hear you say that. I...I still love you too."

"Come here."

"Hot fudge, it feels good to be in your arms again. I missed this, Nick."

"It sure does. Me too."

"And you promise, no more cocoa?"

"I promise. Golly, sugar pie, I want to do *more* than just hug you."

"Now, husband, we can't expect everything to be sunshine and rainbows right away. It will take time and work. We need to—"

"Shh. Just kiss me."

"Mmm. Okay, maybe a tiny rainbow."

"Whaddya say, Mrs. Claus? Do you wanna push the beds together tonight? No use wasting a perfectly good 'Santa sausage.'"

"Oooh, Nick!"

HAPPY ACCIDENTS

"Are you ready to do this?" I asked, buttoning my sport blazer. I looked up at the towering mansion looming before us, its frontage layered with pillars and ornate embellishments. "These two are worth a mint. I mean, Mona's jewellery alone will pay our bills for a year."

Linda rolled her eyes heavenward at the mention of Mona. The independently wealthy and admittedly very attractive woman had regularly frequented the upscale private surgery clinic I once managed. She flirted incessantly while planning her nip and tucks. Then a month ago—ironically, the same day I got fired—she handed me an exclusive invite to her gastronomy club meeting, whispering, *"The food is just foreplay."*

"As ready as I'll ever be," Linda said, her words jarring me from the memory. "But what happens after a year? After what happened, you won't find another job that pays the kind of money we need."

I swept my arm down the street. "Linda. Babe. This is the richest suburb around—believe me, there are plenty other marks."

"Marks? Geez, Don, you're really getting into this. C'mon, we should just suck it up and accept we can't afford this lifestyle anymore. We could barely afford it before."

"No! We've worked too hard to give everything up. Don't worry.

I'll find another job or finally sell my patented bowel clean-out powder. This is just to get us through."

Linda scowled. "That damn powder is what got us into this mess in the first place."

I flashed her a warning look. "Hey, my dad was a respected GI surgeon. He swore this concoction would be revolutionary, and I believe in that. It works great for me!"

Her arms flew up. "You're the exception! That poor guy you slipped it to won't agree—you know, the one suing the clinic because his bowels leaked for weeks?"

"Look, I'm sorry, *okay*? The damn dosage was off, and yes, it threw a wrench into everything, but that won't happen again." I took my wife's hand, squeezing. "Please, just stick to the plan. We need this."

With a sigh, Linda grudgingly nodded. Smoothing the wrinkles out of her retro shirtwaist evening dress, she muttered, "Fine."

MONA GREETED US AT THE DOOR, HER SPEECH SLIGHTLY slurred. "Don, you came! And this is your beautiful wife? Gorgeous." She purred the last line, eyes swiping us both up and down. Linda forced an awkward smile, clutching her mashed potato casserole. The upbeat music and chatter echoing down the hall seemed a little exuberant for this kind of meeting.

"Keys into the bowl there. Don't want any drunk drivers, right?" She winked playfully. I did as she asked. "Now, follow me." Mona led the way down the hall. "You're going to have a great time tonight. This is a delightful group, supportive and caring. Eager to learn what works best."

I grinned, seizing my chance to sound knowledgeable. "Well, I certainly know a lot about what works best—I'm pretty regular. Twice a day without fail. Yep. But it wasn't always that way." Proudly presenting my pouch of bowel cleansing powder, I added, "It's a custom mix. Really potent. With only tiny doses, this gets your whole system working like clockwork."

Spying Linda's eyeroll, I sliced a glare her way.

Mona faltered momentarily, turning around. She stared at the bag of granular white crystals a moment, then broke into excited giggles. "How delightful. Now, I'm extra glad I invited you! We'll save *that* for *later.*" She gave my shoulder a playful slap, carrying on.

The hallway soon opened into a generous kitchen and living area. "Now, make yourselves at home. Mingle. Taste anything you see—remember, gastronomy is only half the fun of these meetings." With a delicate finger wave, Mona sauntered off, and several sets of eyes swung our way, inspecting us like we were up for best in show.

A low growl rumbled in Linda's throat. She hesitantly put her casserole down on the counter, the space already packed with all kinds of fancy-looking food platters. Turning her back on the strangers, her wide eyes locked on mine. "This is a *gastronomy* club?"

"Yeah, I told you that."

She hissed between gritted teeth. "No, you said it was a gastroscopy club."

I popped a cracker littered with colourful blobs into my mouth. "Right. Potato, potato, they're the same thing. Who knew there were clubs dedicated to intestinal scopes?"

Linda's eyes blazed. "No, they're not the same! Gastronomy is—"

"Hello! My wife and I wanted to introduce ourselves." A tall, James Bond-looking fellow and his platinum blond wife eagerly shook our hands. "We're the Schandals. Like *scandal,* but with an 'h.' Luke and Tilly. Lovely to meet you."

Smiling politely, Linda replied, "It's lovely to meet you too. We're Linda and Don."

"Yes, we heard. Did you bring a dish? Goodness, we absolutely *must* try it," Tilly said, leaning in.

Linda shook her head emphatically, moving to block her casserole. "Oh, no, it's nothing really. I-I was really rushed for time."

I looked over, dumbfounded. "Linda, dear, what are you talking about?" I chuckled, wrapping an arm around her shoulders. "She makes the best mashed potatoes. Seriously. Dig in before they're gone." Linda's eyes seared into mine like two hot fire pokers ready to impale.

Luke waved a hand. "I'm sure it's delightful." But after taking a bite, his tight expression belied a less than tickled palette.

Cheeks flushing, Linda rushed to say, "I only use the *finest* Asian garlic and hand-churned butter from Morocco. The unique flavours can be an acquired taste." Confused, I opened my mouth to speak, but Linda's branded glare promptly shut it again—her unspoken warning to zip it received loud and clear.

The couple simply nodded. The *oh, I see* kind.

Tilly lowered her plate and raised her pencil-thin brows. "So, do your exotic tastes extend into *other facets of life?*"

I thought for a moment. "Well, I do enjoy a Heineken now and then."

The couple looked at each other, then burst into laughter. Tilly said, "Oh! Mona didn't tell us how funny you are. I hope the keys swing our way tonight." She smiled with a hunger that wasn't for food. Then the pair continued mingling.

Linda and I both shuffled toward the corner, away from prying ears.

"Um..." I whispered. "What is going on here? These people keep giving us come-hither stares. And what's with the keys?"

She shrugged. "No clue. I mean, check out the guy at 9 o'clock."

I glanced. "Geez, he's practically undressing you with his eyes. I want to punch him."

"You could offer him your poop powder. That'll turn him off." She smirked, then levelled her gaze at me. "I was trying to tell you before—gastronomy is about people delighting in good food. Yet Mona said that's *only half* of this meeting." Linda clucked her tongue, thinking.

"Gastronomy. Huh. Who knew?"

"Most people."

"Whatever. Back on target." I leaned in to whisper. "The sooner we snatch Mona's jewellery, the sooner we can bail."

Linda nodded. "Agreed."

"Say you're going to the *bathroom*, then scope out the bedroom. I'll keep mingling. If the coast is clear, steal the jewels. Necklaces, brooches, tiaras, whatever she's got. If it's not clear, I'll fake a heart attack like we planned."

"Right. Understood." Linda took a steadying breath.

I gave my wife's shaky hand a quick squeeze. "We got this."

Together, we approached the cliques of chatting foodies. It didn't take long before several booze-infused couples converged like buzzards to roadkill. Linda excused herself to the bathroom, leaving me alone to tackle the awkward conversation. I scrambled to answer their bizarre questions.

Do you work out?

What's your favourite spice mix for paella?

What size shoes do you wear?

Moments later, Mona slinked over like a cat on the prowl, sliding her hand around my forearm. She leaned in, her breath reeking of fruity liquor. I felt thankful for her interruption.

"Having a good time, Don?"

I swallowed hard, nodding. "Yes. Absolutely. This is a wonderful meeting *about the deliciousness of food.*" Forcing a smile, my eyes darted between the eager faces surrounding me. "I just love food."

"As do we all. But that's only the appetizer." Her fingers walked up my bicep.

I cleared my throat. "Oh?"

Mona's tipsy husband, who looked like an Arnold Schwarzenegger impersonator, walked over with the bowl of keys. "The fun is just beginning. Next, we get to take turns picking from the bowl. When the keys are gone, we have a swinging good time."

"And what do the keys represent?" Linda asked, appearing out of nowhere. She immediately took my arm back from Mona, an overly pleasant smile plastered on her face.

Mona seemed both irritated she'd been displaced and surprised by the question. "I'm sorry, I thought you understood. We get sexy with the couple who draws our keys. Remember when I told you the food was just foreplay?" She scoffed at first, then broke into giggles.

Others joined in, looking at us like we were a pair of bumbling little kittens.

Swinging...swingers? People still do that?

Linda and I shared a glance—mine of realization, hers of terror. *How can we escape this and still get the jewels?*

Mona must've sensed our hesitation, quickly adding, "But first, let's loosen up. Relax. Have some fun. Don, where's your blow?" She held her hand out to me.

My eyes flicked side to side. "My what now?"

She laughed, abruptly digging into my blazer pocket and brandishing my poop powder. "Don't hold out on us now. Let's do this! Paul?"

Her husband cleared a space on the glass-top coffee table. Mona poured out my special mix while Paul pulled out a credit card and rolled a dollar bill. With obvious skill, he cut a line.

Suddenly realizing what was happening, I stepped forward. "Uh..."

But it was too late. Paul snorted the line, sniffing and coughing a few times. It was then I noticed an odd tattoo poked out from beneath his collared shirt—a bloody skull smoking a joint with two smoking pistols behind. Not exactly an average tattoo choice. Letting out a hoot, he shook his head, teeth bared like a rogue lion. "Now it's a party!"

Everyone laughed, and one by one, couples stepped up to take a hit.

My wife and I quietly retreated, pretending to nibble on food at the kitchen counter. Pouring a glass of wine, Linda downed it and leaned over to whisper, "Oh my God, these people are out of control I mean, should we tell them?"

"I don't know. If they kick us out, we'll have nothing. Did you have any luck when you went snooping?"

"No, someone saw me in the back hallway—this house is huge— I had to make up some story about getting lost trying to find the bathroom."

"Shit." I bit back a groan, pushing food around my plate with a fork.

"But I saw where their bedroom is."

"That's good..."

Linda bit her lip. "Don, maybe we should just go. We can slip out now before they notice. I'm *really* not prepared to get swung tonight."

"What? No. Listen, I can fake the heart attack. I got a standing ovation as *Hamlet* back in high school. We still have a shot." I gave a confident nod.

Mona waved, barking, "You guys, get over here before it's all gone."

Smiling, I waved back. "Oh, no, we're good! We snorted a bunch before we came. We're looped." Mona shook her head, giggling, then turned back to the blow fest.

Linda leaned closer, crossing her arms. "You know, it's kinda rude they just divvied it up and helped themselves, isn't it? I mean, it's *our* fake drugs."

I stared, incredulous. "Is *that* what you're thinking about? You baffle me sometimes."

Moments later, Paul wrangled us back into the group, his meaty fingers pinching my butt. I cringed internally but kept smiling.

Everyone was in good spirits, waiting for the high to kick in.

Or something...

Linda gave me 'the look,' and I was just about to clutch my chest in cardiac distress when the symptoms started. People held their stomachs, faces contorted. Drunken foodies fled for the bathrooms. Sphincteral excretions reverberated around the room as folks doubled over.

"Oh, no," I muttered.

"Are they going to die?" Linda whispered; her eyes wide with panic. She started googling side effects of snorting industrial-strength laxatives on her phone.

Mona glared at us, her face sweaty and pale. "What did you give us?"

What do I say? Flustered and desperate, I blurted the only thing that came to my mind. "Dammit, this was a fresh batch from a new supplier. Bastard must've cut it with something!" Shaking my fist, I kicked the base of the kitchen island.

Mona's eyes grew rounder. "It's bad blow?" Her typically flirty face twisted in anger. She shouted at her husband, who was retching in a wastebasket. "Call the doctor!"

Linda thrust her phone in the air. "I'll call 911!"

Everyone groaned *"No"* at the same time.

Mona growled, "We have our own doctor on call. Don't need police sniffing around."

"Ah, yes...makes sense," I replied, thinking it most certainly did not. But regardless, that boded well for us. I locked eyes with Linda, motioning with my head toward the bedroom.

Her shoulders raised, she mouthed, *really?*

I nodded more forcefully. *Go.* She grudgingly disappeared down the hall while I kept a lookout. A gastric symphony wafted through the air as party-goers ran for anywhere they might purge in peace. I cringed, mourning the once-beautiful carpets.

To be nice, I offered Mona a cup of water. "I'm so sorry, I had no idea!" She glowered up at me. With a nervous chuckle, I continued. "We were really looking forward to, you know, all the swinging."

Mona, now less-than-presentable, shook with rage. "Just get out!"

I backed away as a team of doctors rushed in. Linda, her timing impeccable, reappeared from the hall and flashed a sly grin. Her purse sagged on her slightly tilted frame. Apologizing profusely, my clammy hands fumbled in an attempt to retrieve our keys from the bowl.

"Go!" Mona screamed.

Finally, with a yank, I snared the keys and speed-walked out the door. Linda and I raced home, wasting zero time. We didn't say a word to each other the whole ride, our pensive eyes pinned to the rear-view mirrors. But by the way Linda clutched her purse—like a nervous tourist riding a chicken bus during a popular festival—I knew something good was inside.

My sweaty hands slowly infected my forehead. I wiped the moisture as I obsessively checked our tail for any sign we'd been followed. But there was nothing.

Once home, we hastily locked the doors and windows. Closed all the blinds. Only when we were safe inside our bedroom did Linda finally open her purse.

"So, you got the jewellery?"

My wife beamed. "Better." She pulled out three misshapen gold bars and a thick wad of cash. She unfurled the chunky roll, which also revealed several small papers scribbled with random numbers, scratch marks, and the scrawled words *Smoking Skulls*. My mind flitted back to Paul's tattoo, feeling like I should recognize that name from somewhere...then promptly pushed the thought out of my mind as Linda spread the bills onto the bed next to the bars.

"They must be into some crazy shit. I only took three, but that will be more than enough for us. I doubt they'll even notice a few are gone."

"Holy crap..." I grinned, caressing the smelted gold. "Wait—*only* three? How many were there?" Picking one up, I turned it slowly in my hands, mesmerized.

"A lot. All stashed in the back of their bedroom closet."

"Not even locked in a safe? That's pretty confident." I let out a low whistle. "No wonder they didn't want police around."

"Right? Lucky break for us. Now we just need to figure out how to sell these babies." Linda's lips twitched. "Hey, Don, looks like your poop powder was good for something after all." Linda avoided my eye roll by dashing into the kitchen, swiftly returning with two full wine glasses. Passing one to me, she raised her own in a toast. We shared a victorious smile.

"To happy accidents."

CLICKING

"**Y**ou. Me. Roadhouse. Tonight."

Pinching the phone to my shoulder, I scrunched my nose. "I don't know, Mike. I kinda have plans already." I closed my briefcase and stood.

"What plans?" My best friend sounded shocked and somewhat skeptical on the other end.

"A date."

"Are you serious? It's about time, dude. With who? Your secretary, Chelsea? That girl is fine as hell. I'm jealous but happy for you."

Resisting the urge to laugh, I shook my head, nearly dropping the phone onto the carpet. "No, Mike, it's not Chelsea." The guy had a major crush—yet kept using me as an excuse for why he hadn't mustered enough courage to ask her out. "For the hundredth time, we're just friends."

"Well then, who is it?"

Through the slatted blinds covering my office window, I spied the girl in question waving enthusiastically at me. The get-over-here kind. "Mike, I'll meet you downstairs in five." I collected my briefcase and what remained of a coffee to-go cup and headed to the door.

Chelsea threw her arms in the air as I walked out, leaning back against her desk. "Geez, it's about time. It's after four, Shane. Some of us want to go home."

"Hey, I'm not stopping you. Skedaddle." I laughed, flicking my fingers.

"I will. But...actually, I hung around because I need to show you something. Based on your cheeriness, I assumed you haven't seen it yet." Chelsea held out a crisp newspaper, her expression growing solemn. "Page six. Sorry."

My eyes skimmed over the page, and I stifled a growl as the skin warmed beneath my collar. Chelsea grimaced, knowing the entire story behind my messy and painfully public breakup last year. I took the paper and shoved it under my armpit, scowling. *How dare she?*

Chelsea shook her head. "Don't even worry about it. Lana's just a child throwing a tantrum because you *dared* to dump her. Believe me, there are far better women out there. You made the right choice."

Running a hand through my hair, I nodded. "Thanks."

Barely a beat of silence hit before Chelsea continued. "Soooo... moving on to happier things." She straightened with a bright smile. "What are you up to tonight?"

Someone called to Chelsea from down the hall, and she held up a finger, mouthing *one minute.*

"Nothing crazy. Take a few pictures. Eat a little pizza." I shrugged.

Her eyes flashed with interest. "Ah, so will you be going to that clearing you told me about last week?"

I nodded, flashing a determined grin. "Yep. Tonight's the night. I can feel it."

Chelsea's friend called again, more insistent now. She grabbed her purse off the desk with an apologetic look. "Sorry, I'm late. But tell me all about it later, okay? Text me."

"Will do."

She disappeared with her friend down the hall, and I headed to the elevators. Minutes later, the doors chimed open to reveal a bored-looking Mike. He perked up as I walked out, falling in step beside me. "So, who are you going on a date with? Do I know her?"

Like a dog with a bone. "It's not that kind of date. Not a *her.* Well, actually, there will be one *her* if I'm speaking technically. A mother —and there could be some tiny females, too.*"* I chuckled, waving to Earl at the building's security desk as we passed by.

"Wait, what are you going on about?" Mike's brows furrowed. "Ah, Shane, you're not talking about animals, are you?" His not-so-subtle sigh practically echoed throughout the lobby.

"I am. There's a fox den I've been scoping. The mated pair just had pups."

Mike ran his hands over his face. "What the hell are you doing photographing some little fox family on a Friday night? We've talked about this. You need to get back out there."

I rolled my eyes to the tiled ceiling. "Why would I? Just to get my heart ripped out and smeared all over the floor like last time? Did you see today's paper? Did you see what she said about me?" It was a struggle to keep calm.

We walked outside, passing beneath two sprawling asymmetrical arches.

Rubbing his neck, Mike muttered, "Yeah, I saw it. Dude, she's a straight-up snake. She slithered into your life, sunk her teeth in, then ate you whole." He shook his head as we reached the parking lot. "And now she's regurgitating and chewing on you like cud."

I smirked. *"Cow's* chew cud. That doesn't really fit with your snake analogy."

"Whatever." Mike sliced his hand through the air, facing me. I stopped short. "The point is, you need to forget about her."

"Believe me, I want nothing to do with Lana. But *she* won't let it go." I waved the newspaper, then paused, smiling politely as a group of coworkers passed by. "Remember that Christmas article she wrote about what bad gift giving does to relationships—starring *me* as a shining example? Since when did digital picture frames become a bad thing?"

Mike shrugged. "Seemed like a great present to me."

"Right? Whatever. Doesn't even matter. But *this*—" I tapped a finger on the article. "—is the first of a series. A series! Detailing her horrible dating experiences to help single women know they're not alone. Three-quarters of this first piece is about me."

"C'mon, she could've had similar experiences with another guy." Mike crossed his arms over his chest.

I pointedly read from the article in hushed tones. "The loser cared more about stalking fluffy animals with a camera than he ever cared about me. It was almost creepy. If he put half as much time into learning how to perform in the bedroom as he did into his hobby, we might've had a chance." I closed my eyes, head lolling on my shoulders.

"Yeah. Damn. You going to call the paper to get a retraction?"

"She didn't use my name, so I doubt my complaint would matter. The shit part is, everyone in our circles will know exactly who she's talking about."

Mike slapped my chest. "Well, that's exactly why you need to get back on the horse. Distract yourself. Not all women are controlling and vindictive like Lana. She never let you go anywhere. Hated your photography. Tried to stop you from seeing *me* even. You need to find someone nice, then rub it in that bitch's face." He ground a fist into his palm for emphasis.

I couldn't help but let out a sombre chuckle as we continued toward our vehicles. "Not too sure anyone would want me after that scathing review, but yeah..."

"Nothing she says matters. You. Me. Roadhouse." His fingers flicked between us, eyebrows wiggling up and down before he put his wrap-around sunglasses on. "Tonight."

I grimaced. "I don't know. It'll be dark by the time I get back from the fox den."

As we reached my truck, we split off. Mike turned, walking backwards toward his car several spaces away. With his eyes laser-focused on me, he pointed a finger, not giving up. "The bar never gets hopping until after 11:00pm anyway. C'mon, it's Friday! You need some fun, and I need a wingman. Please?"

Scratching my neck, I hummed. "Okay, fine."

"Perfect!" Mike's lips split into a dimpled grin as he spun around.

Then, waving over his shoulder, he called, "Tell me when you're back."

"Alright." With a sigh, I got into my truck and headed for home.

IT WAS A WARM EVENING. AFTER A QUICK SUPPER OF HOT dogs and canned beans, I gathered my gear and headed out. My target wasn't too far from a dog park at the edge of the city. There was a sprawling forested area just past the fenced boundary with a meadow nestled within. That's where my fox den was.

I walked on a hard-packed trail, a layer of twigs and pebbled rock crunching beneath my footfalls. Nature-loving citizens looking to get away from the hustle and bustle of city life used the area regularly. I passed some picnic tables, then veered down a less worn path leading toward the meadow.

It was dumb luck I'd stumbled upon the den. I took my dog for a walk one night and spotted the fox pair scurrying into their hole. Returning several times to photograph them, I soon realized the female was pregnant, a litter impending. She'd been keeping close to the den, solidifying my belief that pups were inside.

Nearing the meadow's entrance, I stopped to pull the blanket from my backpack and popped a piece of gum into my mouth. Now I was ready.

Stepping as lightly as possible, I crouched low, creeping forward. The clearing had two rounded hills, both sloping gently to where the den was on the far side. Knee-high grass coated the ground, accented with wildflowers of blue, yellow, and pink. A slight breeze rolled the flora like waves. Once I reached my usual spot beside a young tree at the crest of the first hill, I laid the blanket down and settled on top of it. From this vantage point, I could see over the grass while remaining somewhat hidden.

I set up a small tripod securing my DSLR camera, rigged with a telephoto lens. Zooming in, I focused the viewfinder on a large fallen log at the edge of the tree line. At its base, the ground gave way to a burrow. The foxes weren't presenting themselves yet, but if I sat quietly, I hoped they would.

Sunlight filtered through the leafy trees, casting fluttering shadows across everything within reach. It was so peaceful sitting surrounded by stillness and the native sounds of its inhabitants. My love of photography blossomed after taking a class back in college, and I'd been hooked ever since. Selling some images over the last several years helped me create a small network of connections. Nick Nichols was an idol of mine. Publishing in *National Geographic* like him was my ultimate dream. Maybe someday.

For fun, I zoomed in on a pair of blue jays twittering on a nearby branch. As the shutter captured their fluttering wings, a bright glint flashed in the corner of my vision.

Glancing left, I saw a silhouetted form perched on the rise of the next hill. *What the...* It laid low to the ground, not moving. I'd definitely never seen that there before.

Another glint—the glare of a lens.

Shifting my view, I zoomed in.

The silhouette belonged to a person—a woman—holding a camera to her eye. Was she focusing on the same subject? "Shit, I've been scooped," I muttered under my breath. How did she know about the den? What were the chances?

The woman turned her head toward me. Her hair was pulled back into a messy bun, wayward strands gleaming auburn in the light. The breath snagged in my throat. She was pretty. No, not just pretty—beautiful.

I looked away quickly, returning my attention to the fox den. Still no movement there. Probably because this mysterious photographer had honed in on my territory and scared them off. Slightly irritated, I wished I could just shout out to the woman and investigate further, but if I did that, the foxes would vanish for sure. I might as well pack up and go home.

Another glint. Her camera pointed at me, then promptly turned away. She showed no signs of relocating. Hmm... How could I get her to butt out of my photo op? I'd been scouting this den for weeks.

It bothered me that suddenly this random person might steal the glory.

Removing a notepad from my backpack, I slipped the pen from its elastic holder and quietly flipped to a blank page. Shifting in my seat, I scrawled: *What are you doing here?*

I scanned the empty den area once more, then shifted the tripod to face the woman. Securing my camera, I peered through the viewfinder, holding my notebook up.

She wasn't looking.

I held it higher, giving a slow wave. That caught her attention. Her telephoto lens swung in my direction. Holding a neutral expression, I waited for her reaction.

She poked her head out from behind the camera and smiled. My breath caught again; she had a gorgeous smile. Giving my head a shake, I refocused on my irritation. She shouldn't be here.

The woman set her camera down, digging for something beside her. A minute later, she presented a sketchbook. I zoomed in, reading her pencil drawn words.

Fox den. You?

Eyes bright, she enthusiastically pointed toward the burrow, then exchanged the book for her camera.

"A fox den. No kidding," I mumbled dryly, grasping my pen again. Were her eyes blue or green? It was hard to tell.

Yeah. Been scoping it for weeks, I wrote, deciding to give a small smile. No need to be harsh on the girl. Mistakes happen.

Her eyes widened, then her head ducked, her hand writing furiously. *Oh, wow, I didn't realize anyone else would be here. Have I messed up your shoot?*

See, just a mistake. From looking at her, I got the distinct impression she wasn't the mean type. Her expression was kind, inviting. If I asked her to, I bet she'd leave. But then I'd look like a colossal dick. There was no need for that, was there?

Wisps of hair blew about her oval face. She swiped them away and scratched her nose, the skin crinkling as she fought a sneeze. My lips twitched, amused. I *did* want the shot for myself, but in reality, I had no rightful claim to the foxes.

I bent my head to write another note. *No, it's all good. I think there are pups inside. Waiting for them to come out.*

She beamed, reading that, her hands coming together without actually clapping. *Perfect. So cute,* she replied.

Was she talking about me or the foxes? Wait, what was I thinking? Of course, she was talking about the foxes. I grinned, flashing a thumbs up.

Oh, the foxes! My eyes darted back to the den, barely catching the white tip of a furry tail disappearing inside the hole. Damn. This girl was distracting me. "C'mon, little ones. Come out to play," I whispered. Any minute now, they could come bounding out again. But after several minutes passed with no action, I swiveled back to spy on my new friend.

She was bent over her sketchbook. Every so often, she'd check the viewfinder, then return to whatever she was working on. Was she an artist as well as a photographer?

I peered past her, noticing a wall of angry-looking clouds creeping in from the west. When I looked back, her camera was trained on me this time. She presented a shy smile, and my face flushed, the heat warming all the way to my ears. Averting my gaze, I inspected the folds of my shirt.

Struggling with what to do next, I sensed movement from her hilltop. She'd raised her book in the air. I quickly peered through the lens, a chuckle escaping my lips. The intriguing woman had drawn a picture of me in pencil from her vantage point. It was pretty good.

"So, you *are* an artist..."

I scribbled a new message, my stomach doing a leap as I presented it. *You're very talented. I'm Shane. What's your name?*

As I waited for her response, a low rumble signalled in the distance. As if on cue, the wind kicked up, flipping my page. Those clouds were rolling in quicker than expected. Perhaps tonight might not be the night to see the pups.

Her book was back up. I zoomed in.

Thank you. I'm Ronnie.

"Ronnie. Cute." Was that short for Veronica? Did I know any Veronicas in the photography world? As I wracked my brain, a bolt of lightning fizzled through the darkening sky. A raindrop splattered on my notebook, another landing on my shoulder. The foxes were nowhere to be seen. Though disappointed, I shrugged, unable to argue with nature.

Glancing back over at Ronnie, I noticed she was packing her gear. My heart suddenly hammered in my chest, worried this gorgeous woman might disappear forever. I really wanted to continue getting to know her.

Hoping I didn't sound too forward, I wrote one last note, holding it up. Another crack of thunder boomed after a snake of lightning bit into the ground. More raindrops. I waved urgently, trying to get her attention. Ronnie was busy tucking her camera away when she finally noticed, did a double take, then quickly hoisted her lens.

I'd love to see your pictures sometime. Can I call you?

Swiftly placing the camera back into her bag, Ronnie bent over papers yet again. I held a hand over my lens, trying to shield it from the increasing barrage of moisture showering down. As I swallowed hard, my finger hovered over the shutter, ready.

Seconds later, she jerked the sketchbook into the air, furiously pointing to it as a bolt of electric energy blazed behind her. I didn't waste any time.

Click, click, click.

"Got it." I flashed Ronnie another thumbs up. With that, she stuffed the book into her bag, gave a little wave, and darted into the bush. Collapsing my tripod, I swiftly thrust the blanket and camera within the safety of my pack. More lightning sliced beyond the tree line, making me flinch. Tripod in hand, I ran down the trail.

By the time I reached the truck, my clothes were drenched. I sloshed into the cab, giving my sopping hair a shake, and started laughing. What a mess. Thankful for the waterproof lining in my backpack, I used the blanket to dry my hands and face. Then I retrieved the camera, opening the image gallery. There she was, hair blowing in the wind while holding her paper up... but it was blurry. The damn lightning must've confused the focus. I switched to the next shot. Less blurry, but I still couldn't make out the writing.

"C'mon, c'mon," I begged. Pinching my eyes shut, I willed the last picture to be clear. Swallowing hard, I pressed the *next* button and re-opened my eyes. A readable image welcomed me—seven big numbers displayed across the paper. Her phone number.

Slapping my palm against the steering wheel, I grinned. "Yes!"

LATER THAT NIGHT, I PACED BACK AND FORTH, DEBATING what to do. "Should I call her, Frank?" My German Shepherd sat on his bed—a reliable sounding board. "Or just text maybe? I don't want to seem too desperate. Plus, it's after 10pm. She could be in bed already."

Frank yawned, top lip snagging on his canines to create a bewildered expression.

I smirked, running a hand through my hair. "Well, you're no help."

Mike would swing by any minute to drag me off to the bar. I really wasn't in the mood to go, but the guy had his heart set. He'd never let me back out now. The pacing escalated until, finally, I slapped my own cheek. "Snap out of it, man."

I looked back to Frank, who was busy gnawing on his front paw. "I should just keep it casual and send a text. Yeah?" He groaned and leaned to the side, contorting to sniff his butt. "I'll take that as a yes," I muttered, turning away. After breathing in deep and exhaling loudly, I punched a message into my phone.

S: Hey, it's Shane. From the fox den. It was nice to meet you today.

"And...*send*. There. Super casual." Frank stared blankly, ear twitching. Giving him a scratch, I couldn't help but laugh. "Appreciate your support, buddy."

Several agonizing minutes passed before I heard a notification chime. The screen lit up, and I swiped, biting my lip. Then my shoulders sagged as I read Mike's message.

M: Dude, I'm outside.
S: Okay. Be down in 5.

Wandering into the bathroom, I checked my reflection. I'd donned blue jeans and a navy collared shirt. My short hair looked a bit messy, but wasn't that the style these days, anyway? I shrugged. It was as good as it would get.

Checking my phone, there was still no reply from Ronnie. I grabbed my coat, walking out the door when a chime sounded again. Likely Mike giving me crap for taking so long.

R: Hi! It was nice to meet you too. A pleasant surprise.

I fist pumped. Somewhere in the back of my mind, I was worried she'd given me a fake number. After locking the apartment door, my fingers fumbled about the keyboard.

S: Listen, one of my buddies is dragging me to the Roadhouse tonight. Heading there now. If you have nothing else to do tonight, you should swing by. I'd love to chat more.

Then I wondered if she might feel nervous about meeting me alone.

S: Bring a friend or a group. Whichever.

Heading down the stairs, I swooped through the revolving door. Mike had parked his sports car at the curb. A new message chimed, and I immediately stopped to check it.

R: Maybe. 😉

I grinned. "That's not a no."

Mike impatiently waved me toward the car, and I held my pointer finger up.

S: I look forward to "maybe" seeing you. 😊

Not even a second after I hit send, a wave of insecurity rippled through me. *Was that super cheesy?* I groaned internally, then gave my head a shake, trying to brush it off. Too late now.

I slid into the passenger seat, and Mike pulled onto the street. "Who were you texting?" he asked.

As I clicked my seatbelt into place, I couldn't contain my exuberance. "I might have a date tonight."

Mike's sidelong glance was laced with skepticism. "Real or furry this time?"

"Shut up." I punched his arm, and he recoiled with a laugh. "Real."

Mike's head bopped to the hip hop music pounding from the speakers. "Sweet! Is it Chelsea? Did I mention that girl is fine?"

"Yeah—a few times. Enough about her already!" I shook my head, resting an elbow on the window frame. "No, I met someone today. A photographer. She *might* meet me at the bar." I smiled, feeling good.

"Well, damn." He pounded my fist. "Guess I get to be *your* wingman tonight."

IT WAS ALMOST MIDNIGHT. I'D BEEN KEEPING MY EYES ON the doorway since we arrived. Still no sign of Ronnie. Standing by the bar, I conversed politely while Mike flirted with two girls. Dressed to impress, they both wore short skirts and low-cut tops. A little too much makeup for my taste, but neither woman was unattractive.

My neck stretched to scour another of the many groups walking in, and Mike shot me an elbow, his silent signal telling me to get my head in the game. He'd already advised me to let it go—this *Ronnie* obviously wasn't coming.

Swallowing a sigh, I refocused my attention on the conversation at hand. A raven-haired woman named Sadie regaled Mike with a tale of how her Pomeranian had chewed her most expensive pair of heels.

Mindy—a platinum blonde—leaned into me. "What about you, handsome? What do you do for a living?"

"I work in marketing with Mike." My eyes flicked to the Ronnie-less door, disappointed yet again. If she'd planned on coming, she should've arrived by now...

Mindy's finger traced the curve of my bicep, and I shifted slightly, clearing my throat. "You know, you should really get to know Mike. Great guy. He's been keeping me company while I wait for my girlfriend." I didn't enjoy lying as a rule, but my mind was focused elsewhere.

Her finger stilled, smile faltering. "Oh..." Sipping her drink, she stepped back, scanning for new targets.

Just then, a familiar face walked through the door, and my mood brightened. It was Chelsea. She presented her I.D. to the bouncer, paid the cover, then turned to wait for someone else. It was surprising to see her here. From everything she'd ever said to me, I firmly believed she despised bars—or "meat markets," as she affectionately referred to them.

I poked Mike in the shoulder. He brushed me off, but I ignored the attempt, leaning in to whisper, "Chelsea's here." I winked. My friend's eyes widened momentarily, then flicked to the door. Watching his reaction was more entertaining than old reruns of *Friends*. I grinned as his body slowly inched away from the flirtatious Sadie.

"Excuse us, ladies." Mike smiled graciously. "We need to talk to a friend who just walked in. Catch up with you later." It was a hollow promise but softened the blow.

Slipping out of Sadie's reach, Mike motioned for me to follow. Once safely out of earshot, he spun to face me, running a hand through his hair and cracking his neck like a boxer going into the ring. He checked his breath. "Do I look alright?" The guy actually looked nervous.

"Yeah, you look fine. So, you're *finally* going to ask her out?" He'd had plenty of chances to make meaningful contact at the office but chickened out every single time.

"Think she'll dig me?" He sliced a hand between us. "And you're one hundred percent sure you're *not* into her?"

I laughed, patting his shoulder. "How many times do I need to say there's nothing romantic between us? She's all yours." I pointed to the door. "Go get her."

"Okay. You're my wingman on this." Mike took a deep breath, walking forward.

"Of course."

There were three more women dancing around Chelsea now, each of them trying and failing to get her to dance with them. A flash of auburn hair caught my attention. Craning my neck to get a better look, my breath halted for the third time in one day.

There she was. Ronnie. Her hair fell in waves at her shoulders. She wore fitted skinny jeans and a sparkly black top that showed just enough skin to make a guy take notice. Suddenly I was scrabbling to smooth my shirt and pop a piece of gum in my mouth.

Ronnie belted out a laugh with Chelsea and the others as we approached. I still couldn't believe they knew each other. What a small world. Perhaps too small?

In the next moment, Ronnie stepped back to scan the crowd, clearly looking for someone. Hopefully, for me. As we neared, her eyes landed on mine. A smile lit her face, and my heart did a flip-flop. The gentle curve of her lips captivated me, drew me in. I gave a nervous wave.

Then my ex walked in.

With my proximity being so close to the door, Lana spotted me immediately. I swallowed a low groan as she approached, smirking wickedly and twittering with her friends.

"Did you enjoy reading my column today, Shane?" Lana asked.

With a frown, I replied evenly, "Yes, the lies were skillfully written."

I couldn't help but notice Ronnie watching and whispering with Chelsea from the corner of my eye. My heart sunk. What would she think of me seeing this icy exchange?

Mike glowered at the woman in my defence, which Lana promptly returned with gusto.

Lana raised a finger. "Well, if you—"

Ronnie silenced my ex's words by slipping between us and grabbing my hands with a coquettish smile. "Come dance with me, babe!" She levelled a pointed glare at Lana before dragging me away, affording me zero time to react. However, the sound of Lana's indignant huff fading behind us brought a smile to my face. Once we'd successfully escaped to the dancefloor, my copper-haired saviour gave my hands a squeeze before letting them go. Still recovering from my shock, I awkwardly shuffled my feet, speechless, as I watched her body sway to the music.

The others joined us on the floor, and Mike appeared at my side. He nudged my arm and spoke over the pounding music, just loud enough for me to hear. "So, I take it that's your girl?"

I nodded once, gaze unwavering from my dance partner.

"Dude. Nicely done."

THE EVENING PASSED QUICKLY. OUR GROUP SNAPPED UP A table, shouting and laughing over the music. Whenever the opportunity presented itself, I chatted with Ronnie. I couldn't explain why, but I felt comfortable with her, like we'd known each other for years. But what clinched my interest was how her nose crinkled adorably whenever she laughed, just like it had in the meadow. It turned out she'd been friends with Chelsea since college. She worked as an artsy freelance photographer specializing in portraiture while dabbling with wildlife.

And I'd been right—Ronnie *was* short for Veronica.

When I got Chelsea alone for a minute, I gave her crap for not setting us up sooner. She just shrugged and winked before turning back to Mike, who'd somehow managed to captivate her attention. For a guy who was normally smooth with the ladies, he'd been shy and stuttering around Chelsea. I worried he'd crash and burn, but Chelsea seemed there for it.

Lana had kept her distance, too, which gave me hope she'd finally move on.

Only when patrons in various stages of inebriation began filtering out the doors did I realize 2:00am had rolled around, and the bar was closing for the night. Mike guzzled the last of his beer while the ladies in our party planned to split a cab and head home.

"Are you coming, Ronnie?" Chelsea asked as she donned her coat. With a playfully arched eyebrow, she added, "Or are you *walking* home?"

Ronnie glanced between us, then shook her head with a smile.

"No, I don't live very far from here. I think I'll just walk." She finished the last few sips of her drink.

"I can walk you home," I offered over-enthusiastically, then quickly added in a much cooler tone, "You really shouldn't walk alone at night." Mike gave me an approving nod.

"Sure, thanks." Ronnie stood, and I held out her coat. Slipping her arms in, she shrugged it in place, that nose crinkling again. Flutters invaded my stomach for the millionth time.

Chelsea turned to Mike, placing a quick kiss on his cheek. His eyes lit up—practically glowing with delight. She casually passed him a business card and squeezed his forearm. "Call me." With a wave, she and her friends headed for the door.

"I will," he mumbled, watching her go.

Chuckling, I gave his shoulder a punch. "Oh, man, you got it bad."

Mike punched me right back, but his scowl morphed into a grin. Then he clapped his hands. "Alright, well, I'm outta here. You two sure you're good?" When we both nodded, Mike flashed a sly smile and tipped an invisible hat. "Kay, have fun."

STROLLING DOWN THE SIDEWALK IN THE COOL NIGHT AIR, I dared to be bold and reached for Ronnie's hand. Her skin felt warm, and without hesitation, she laced her fingers through mine.

"Soooo…" Feeling much lighter on my feet, I swung our arms between us. "How did you *really* find out about the fox den?" The moon was out and cast a muted glow across her face.

"Well…" Her coy smile said it all.

Leaning my head back, I groaned. "It was Chelsea."

Ronnie bounded in front of me, still holding my hand as she walked backward. "It was. But I swear I had no clue you were going to be there at the meadow. She gave me the tip a few days ago—saying she'd seen a den while out walking, which I know now was a blatant lie. She insisted I check it out *today*."

My eyes narrowed as I grasped her other hand, loving how natural it felt. "That sneaky woman... You know, I suspected it the moment I saw you two together. I hadn't told many people about the den."

"I know you guys are close. She's talked about you before." She fell back in step beside me. "I think it's great you two get to work together. I bet that's so much fun." Her eyes grew solemn. "I moved around a lot as a kid—military family—so making and *keeping* friends was hard. Thankfully, I met Chelsea in college, and we've been close ever since."

"Yeah, she's pretty great." I shoved my free hand into the pocket of my jeans, then ripped it out again. "But we're not *that* close. I mean, it's never been romantic or anything. She's like a sister to me."

Ronnie laughed, nudging my side. "I know."

"Good," I said, relieved. Then the corners of my mouth lifted sympathetically. "Man, that must've been tough moving around all the time."

"It was sometimes, but I also got to travel a lot. I learned a lot about the world. There are pros and cons to everything, right?" She shrugged, a quiet strength showing in her expression.

"That's a good way to look at it." Our hands separated briefly as we passed around a lamppost before finding their way back together again. "Oh, and thanks for saving me back there, you know, with my ex... I assume Chelsea must've filled you in?" She had to have. Why else would Ronnie have done what she did back in the bar? I didn't particularly want to talk about Lana right now, but I was really vibing this girl and wanted nothing chasing her away.

"You're welcome." She squeezed my hand, nodding. "And all Chelsea said was that a good friend of hers—this *Shane* fellow—got hurt pretty bad and that he was a great guy who didn't deserve it. So far, I must say I agree with her." Ronnie cast a flirty glance my way, her emerald irises glistening in the lamplight. "And, whenever you need saving, just let me know."

Heat flamed in my cheeks; the pink was probably visible from space. "I'm glad to hear that."

My heart rate probably doubled as we approached her apartment building. We stopped beside the concrete steps, and I swallowed hard, the simple act requiring twice the effort it should've. "I had lots of fun tonight. I'm really glad you decided to come out." As I nervously rubbed my arm, my gaze locked with hers. "Honestly, I couldn't get you off my mind after the meadow."

"Me too, on all counts." Her voice was a soft caress as she inched closer.

I leaned down to kiss her cheek, but when I pulled back, Ronnie slipped a hand around my neck and guided my mouth to hers. The kiss was warm and sweet, her lips silken as they pressed against mine. Her fingers threaded through the hair at the nape of my neck. My hands settled about her waist as I breathed in her perfume, wishing this moment would never end.

When our lips finally parted, I backed away with a bashful chuckle.

"Until next time," I murmured and grudgingly released her.

Ronnie climbed the stairs, then turned, a sudden mischief flashing in her eyes. Digging through her purse, she revealed a small notepad similar to the one I always carried. After scribbling something in pen, she held it up for me to see. ***Meet at the fox den tomorrow?***

Her smile beamed, and I knew this woman would be trouble in a very good way.

I grinned. "My hill or yours?"

ACKNOWLEDGMENTS

Thank you to all the readers who took a chance on picking up this book. There'd be zero point in doing what I do without you. And I *love* doing it, so your support means the world to me.

This book has been in the works for quite a while. The stories you've read encompass years of writing—from 2019, when I dove headlong back into my childhood writing passion, all the way into 2022. Some stories were birthed through writing competitions, while others simply bloomed in my mind, demanding to be written. Several pieces have been previously published, others have won or placed in contests, while a few are new, never-before-seen tales for you to enjoy.

I've had an incredible writing journey thus far, but I definitely didn't travel alone. They say it takes a village to raise a child. Well, I feel the same is true of a writer's dream. So many lovely people have generously uplifted or assisted me along the way, and in creating these specific stories. I will try to thank those people, but please accept my sincerest apologies if I miss anyone. My memory is sadly imperfect, but that doesn't lessen the value of the kindness you've shared with me by any measure.

Firstly, thanks to my amazing husband, Steve Clarke, who lets me bounce ideas off him endlessly (and puts up with my creative mood swings), and to my two beautiful sons Eithan and Austin, who constantly inspire me in so many ways. Thanks to my mother-in-law Marg Clarke for reading many of these stories and for giving her unfailing support. Thanks to the Night Writers, my local writing group, for their encouragement. Thank you to WAB (Write Around the Block), an online writing group I am part of, who've seen most of these stories in various stages of completion. Now, I didn't always keep good records, but I'd like to highlight the folks I've confirmed critiqued any number of stories or elements of this book: Karlynn Sievers, Sue Cook, Holly Rae Garcia, Lauren Voeltz, TE Bradford, Melinda Hagenson, Talia Camozzi, Sharon Kretschmer, Lin Morris, Lisa Kannegiesser Short, Elizabeth Hakken Candido, Roni Piplani-Schienvar, Heather Lander, Janice Johnson, Angela Teagardner, Lisa Fox, Andrea Goyan, Connie Chang, Nikki Ervice, Briana Shucart, Kerry A. Waight, EJ Sidle, Kimberly DeLeon, Laurie Hicks, Renee Boyer, Regan Puckett, Emily Roth, John Adams, Mark Kramarzewski, Alex Otto.

I'd like to offer a special shout out to Josie Thwaits-Queen, who helped me get this collection into shape and gave me the confidence to believe people might actually like reading it.

My thanks also go out to everyone in my own Facebook community Write State of Mind, and of course, my amazing launch team (go Launchables!), with special mentions for Rosa Rawlings, Holly Rae Garcia, Robert Beech, Karlynn Sievers, Kim Hart, Jennifer Lynn Ikner Marin, TE Bradford, Chad Klein, Angela Teagardner, Laurie Carmody, Corinna Grenier, Karen May, Janna Tinley Miller, Iris Jones, and Lisa Flower. You guys have been so uplifting and generous in your willingness to help me out. I'll be forever grateful.

I'd like to give special gratitude to everyone who took the time to read an advanced copy and honoured me with a review. Thanks to my editor Charlie Knight, and my interior/ebook formatter Steven Pajak. I'm thankful to all the publications who believed in my writing enough to publish some of these pieces well in advance of this book.

Last, but not least, thank you to the members of my extended family who've encouraged my writing in some way—big or small—including my Grandma (Ruby) and Grandpa (Bill) Rempel, aunt Sylvia Klassen, cousin Roxanne Hillman, nephew Rylan McKenzie, sister Kathy McKenzie, and my parents Jerry and Connie Rempel.

Whew! I think that just about does it. Goodness, I can't believe this is the very end of the book. Well, I guess that just means I'll have to start working on another.

I'd like to share one parting thought... It's my sincerest hope that this collection gave you a smile. If it did, please take a moment of your day to leave a review online and help get more lips twitching. Reach out to me via any of my social media, too. I'd love to hear from you.

Best wishes,

R.A. Clarke

ABOUT THE AUTHOR

 R.A. Clarke is a former police officer turned stay-at-home mom from Portage la Prairie, MB. She shares life with a sport-aholic husband, two adorable children, and an ever-expanding collection of novels-in-progress. Besides sipping coffee and escaping to the lake, R.A. enjoys plotting multi-genre short fiction, and also writes/illustrates children's chapter books as Rachael Clarke. She has won international short story competitions such as The Writer's Games, Writer's Weekly, and Red Penguin Books humour contest. In 2021, she was named a Hindi's Libraries Females of Fiction finalist, a Dark Sire Award finalist, and a Futurescapes Award finalist. R.A.'s work has been published by a variety of publications, including Sinister Smile Press, Cloaked Press LLC, and Polar Borealis Magazine, among others.

Follow her at: www.rachaelclarkewrites.com.
Instagram: @rachaelclarkewrites
Facebook: https://www.facebook.com/raclarkeauthor
Twitter: @raclarkewrites

PRIOR PUBLICATION ACCREDITATION

A FRIEND IN NEED – 2020 Writer's Games contest anthology *72 Hours of Insanity, Anthology of The Games, vol 9*. Placed third in a contest heat.

DON'T POP TIL' YOU GET ENOUGH – 2019 Our Town, *A Collection of Canadian Short Stories* by Polar Expressions Publishing.

PINCHING PENNIES – 2019 Writer's Games contest anthology *72 Hours of Insanity, Anthology of The Games, vol 7*. Placed first in a contest heat.

TO FLUFF OR NOT TO FLUFF – 2019 Published on R.A. Clarke's blog at www.rachaelclarkeauthor.com (this site is no longer active).

MR. REGRET – *Fall Into Fantasy*, 2020 Edition by Cloaked Press LLC.

HAPPY ACCIDENTS – 2022 *Happy Accidents*, and other humorous short stories by Red Penguin Books. Contest winning story.

CLICKING – 2020 Writer's Games contest anthology *72 Hours of Insanity, Anthology of The Games, vol 9*. Placed second in a contest heat. 2022 *Love Wins Ukraine Charity Anthology* (reprint).

MORE FROM R.A. CLARKE

52 original speculative fiction prompts to inspire and spark your creative flame. Spin, switch, expand, elevate, and transform these concepts into your own. Oh, and don't forget to have fun while you're at it. Are you ready to dive in and write that next great story?

Available wherever books are sold.

www.pageturnpress.com

Made in the USA
Las Vegas, NV
13 January 2023

65563319R00116